THE ENTROPY
OF LOSS

NP Novellas:

THE ENTROPY OF LOSS

Stewart Hotston

NewCon Press
England

First published in the UK April 2022 by
NewCon Press
41 Wheatsheaf Road,
Alconbury Weston,
Cambs, PE28 4LF

NPN019 (limited edition hardback)
NPN020 (paperback)

10 9 8 7 6 5 4 3 2 1

ISBN:

978-1-914953-18-7 (hardback)
978-1-914953-19-4 (paperback)

Cover layout and design by Ian Whates

Typesetting and editorial meddling by Ian Whates
Text layout by Ian Whates

Part 1 – Denial

One

We were beyond consultants, beyond MRIs, beyond phlebotomy. Oncology was reduced to information without hope. On the plus side, her hair was growing back now the treatments had stopped, as thin as silk but with none of the lustre. After three years of stalling, the sand in her hourglass was measured now in days and hours. Minutes.

A pot of jelly sat warming on the side table next to her bed. I'd slurp it down without thinking at some point in case the nurse came by to demand Rhona finish up. I was done forcing her to do anything.

They say that knowing death's coming allows you to prepare.

That's bullshit.

I still sat at home thinking about all we wanted to do, the places we'd be going on holiday, the review of a new restaurant at which we were going to eat.

The sharpened stones that had grown in my stomach at the thought of a world without her cut at me but I couldn't accept they were telling the truth.

'Tell me about it again.' Her voice sounded like tissue paper being torn and I worried she was reaching her limit for the day. The light in the room was soft and yellow, heavy with golden hints from the setting sun.

Rhona refused to slip the blinds, insisting sunshine in the UK was rare enough that when it deigned to shine upon us we had a duty to let it in. So the walls were bleached an inflamed bronze as a last echo of dying light, fat with promises that couldn't be held together.

I had my back to its brilliance, facing her bed. She was sitting upright, the blankets folded back so they only covered her feet. Even with the door to her room open I couldn't hear the sounds of other residents. A cleaner had passed by half an hour ago, the whispering swish of their brush the only intrusion.

I got lost remembering the days before she'd moved into the hospice, how I'd been suspicious that anywhere could be as comfortable as home. Except I realised quickly enough the care she received was far beyond anything I could provide. A standard to which my broken, tired heart couldn't reach.

Somewhere darker I understood how it was respite for me as well, how not having her at home meant I had moments in which I could sleep, shit or unravel in front of the television. It meant I didn't have to be on call every hour of every day.

I felt guilty even though none of it was my fault.

'Sarah,' said Rhona, calling me back to the room.

I blinked, not sure how much I'd missed. I wanted to cry but wouldn't. Not in front of her. She had enough to deal with without seeing how much I was going to miss her. I gulped down the emotion which had travelled up from my stomach and into my throat, pushing it down hard until I felt I could look her in the face without it scything out of my eyes.

'The question, tell me about it again,' she said, taking hold of my hand.

I nodded dumbly for a moment. I wanted to ask if this was how she wished to spend her remaining days. Except I knew she'd tell me it was.

'Can't I just recite some Donne?'

'The question!' she insisted.

'Information is fundamental. Information theory makes common sense precise,' I said, but she rolled her eyes and huffed impatiently.

'I don't need the dinner party speech, Sarah. I already know you're brilliant.'

I tried again. 'If you had a biased coin how would you figure out how biased it was?'

'You asked that at the interview?' Rhona looked appalled.

'They're kids with degrees from Harvard, Oxbridge. They should be able to do it standing on their heads. One of them guessed ten.' I laughed at the nonsense of it. 'Ten! As if a number was the answer.

Even once you figure it out that's woefully too small for any case worth thinking about.'

'I hope you didn't laugh at them,' she said.

'Of course not,' I said, frightened she thought I was capable of such callousness. 'They knew it wasn't going well without me telling them.'

A quiet grew between us. I was caught by the possibility I was exactly as cruel as she'd suggested. In moments since she'd been diagnosed I noticed a detachment to my behaviour, an unwillingness to consider other people's troubles as comparable to mine and Rhona's. There had been a female undergrad interning with us who'd cried when she couldn't understand what I was trying to show her, some basic bit of coding. I was toxically impatient I realised later, but in the moment when the tears started rolling I told her that waterworks might work with my male colleagues but I wasn't moved. I told her she needed to stop crying and spend her energy on thinking instead.

Rhona looked at me and I could see we both knew it was me who'd reached my limit today.

'I had an idea for a new series of pieces,' she said, as if she'd been in the studio all day.

'I want to hear all about it,' I said, grateful for the reprieve.

'It's about what life would be if we weren't interpreting everything we see. I thought about showing a series of images which can't be recognised, close ups, shots from too far away, or obscured in such a way that the observer can't work out what they're looking at.'

'You know they'll spend all their time trying,' I said, thinking of people standing in front of images with their heads tilted to one side while they guessed at what they were seeing.

She smiled, a dagger of fragile flame cutting at my soul. 'The commentary is the important bit. I'd present them with names like "watermelon sunset".'

I laughed despite myself.

'That's good,' she said, possibly at my laughter. 'They'd be trying to see bright pink watermelon flesh while they were really looking at an image of half a calf's tongue photographed with an infrared filter.

The point is I want to highlight how their interpretation won't help them understand what they're seeing. That they're not seeing what's there because they're trying so hard to see what's there.'

I stroked the back of her hand, sensitive to the paper thinness of her skin. How its whiteness had shaded to yellow, how it looked like chicken skin when contrasted with the hazelnut brown of my own hand. 'And you call me mean.'

'What does yours help people do?' She asked, the words stopping my fading giggles. She saw my face, understood I'd taken it the wrong way. 'I mean, why do you ask them those questions? Surely you know whether they're any good before you decide to meet them. Couldn't you ask them something useful? Something that would help them understand what you need.'

My cheeks felt heavy, as if someone were pushing down on my cheekbones with their fingertips. A jumble of words waltzed around my mouth but none of them could find the exit.

The splattered gold of the sunset faded, pulling its metallic fire from the walls as if it were melting into darkness. I watched it decay and waited for the noise in my head to still.

We were saved from ourselves when the phone in my pocket buzzed. Without commenting I stood, turning away from the bed to look out of the window.

'Hi? It's me, Akshai. Is now a bad time?' said the voice on the other end.

I sighed. 'It's fine. How can I help, Akshai?'

'There's something wrong with the simulation. When are you coming in, it's just that I don't want to lose everything or stop it now if it's actually okay.'

'You're sure it's not a bug or something equally trivial?'

'Nothing's coming up on the debugging tools.' She paused. 'If there is, it's deep in the logic trees and I can't see what's driving the error without stopping the run. Do you want me to stop the run?' I knew she wanted me to take responsibility for the situation, but I wasn't even on site.

'For now, leave it to run. It won't hurt to let it alone for now.'

'When will you be here?' She asked.

'I'll be there in an hour.' I said it loudly enough Rhona would know there was no debate to be had, although it wasn't her I intended to convince.

Done with Akshai, I turned back to Rhona. She was reclined with eyes closed.

'My love,' I said. Her eyelids fluttered; she was awake. 'I've got to go. Akshai's having a meltdown and is threatening to switch off the entire project if I don't go back.'

'You told her to leave it alone,' she whispered, her face still, her eyes staying shut.

I rolled my shoulders, a gesture she couldn't see. 'She'll worry about it until I'm there.' I stood in the room, my palms itching. Eventually Rhona nodded. Like a woman discovering yet another man was a friend because they wanted something more than friendship.

'Fine,' she said quietly, her voice as soft as the brushes on the door in the moment when it shut tight against the doorframe.

I kissed her on the forehead, my hand touching her cheek as I did so. We were good at pretending there was nothing wrong.

I spent the half hour in the car listening to the radio, some talking heads where there was zero chance of them playing music which could trigger tears. Had I left too quickly? Would Rhona make me pay for it tomorrow when I went to see her? I decided I'd be good, would refresh her library with new audio books when I eventually got home.

I assumed Akshai had made a stupid mistake. I imagined the embarrassed look on her face when I walked in, sat down and immediately saw the issue as it leapt out from the screen.

It would be good to fix something like that. I realised I'd enjoy solving the problem even more if it took a long while. I didn't relish the prospect of being there well past dinner time, but I didn't truly resent the possibility either.

What was I supposed to do at home on my own? I don't think I'd ever been to the pool as often as in the last few months. I'd developed a single muscle on both arms where I insisted on length after length of front crawl. I often stood looking at my body after getting out of the pool, towel in my hand so it wouldn't fall on the floor, wishing there was just a little more definition to show elsewhere for all the miles being logged. It was maddening to share a lane with anyone and bitterly ironic to find the satisfaction of such sought-after loneliness was peculiarly specific to swimming; there was no mapping how good being alone in the pool felt against arriving at home in the dark to find myself a soul bubbling around with no one to bump into.

I parked underneath a young London Plane tree whose leaves broke the white of the car park's lights. Stooping to take one of the broad leaves from the tarmac, my fingers peeled back the skein vein by vein as I walked past security and into the lab, finally waving the skeletal stalk against lips that had forgotten the feel of Rhona's skin.

I couldn't find Akshai and was greeted by a note on my desk explaining that she'd gone to the gym and would be back at about the time I arrived.

She was very bright but, as if to compensate, her sense of time was terrible and I knew better than to wait around like a dog for its master.

There was a knock on my office door half an hour later. Akshai came in without waiting, which I had always encouraged her to do; it was the company who insisted I have a separate office in the first place and training my staff to ignore what that implied was the best act of rebellion I could serve up.

I asked if she'd had her hair cut.

'It's just wet,' she said, and looked embarrassed.

'I made better time than I anticipated.' We both knew there was nothing she needed me for so urgently that I'd had to leave Rhona as soon as I'd taken the call. The thought scanned across my mind that she was too young to understand why I'd left immediately, but then we're all too young to deal with death.

'Do you want to show me what's going on?'

'Oh. Yes,' she said, her wide eyes sliding into focus as her anxiety about talking to me faded. 'I've been over the normal culprits, but they're all innocent.'

'You've checked with the sys admin at the data centre?' Our equivalent of turning it off and on again as I would tell Rhona.

12

She nodded, not taking offence at such a school girl question. 'Pat said the network was working fine and our nodes were all nominal.'

'Whatever it is, the problem's in the code.'

Another nod, more emphatic this time. 'It has to be. The numbers are coming out all wrong.'

'How many black holes are you running?'

'It's a large sample,' she said, hesitating and proud. I waited for her to tell me the exact number. 'A hundred thousand.'

She was right to be proud; it was the largest sample size we'd run by a factor of three. I stood up, grabbing my tablet as I did so. 'Let's go see. Tell me what you did to reach that number.'

We stalked across to the lab through a building lit with sickly blue white strip lights which gave the grey walls the feel of brain matter.

The lab was in an Annexe built entirely to house the computational network we were using for our experiments. It connected to the rest of the facility via a short corridor ending in a security sealed entrance. The company was interested in encryption but our work, my ideas, were the ones deemed most likely to create encryption no one could break. Other projects had come and gone in the two years I'd been there. It was hardly what I'd thought research would be like; I spent my postgrad years working in global teams of hundreds where the joke was how the names on our papers took up as much space as the actual content.

Akshai was what the company desired; a smart mathematician who worked on her own, happy to sit at a poorly lit desk on a cheap chair for days on end while she figured out a new transformation in Hilbert space by hand.

We passed through electronic locks which kept even company members out of the Annexe and into a temperature controlled world. The physical landscape of the lab hid worlds beyond count folded upon themselves by fundamental possibilities.

Except Akshai managed to rip the glamour out of that idea with discarded takeaway cartons. A ripe, meaty perfume greeted us as the door opened. Looking over at Akshai, it was clear she didn't notice.

'You had curry for dinner last night?' I asked, hoping I was being diplomatic but not too subtle.

'How did you know?' She asked.

At which point I decided being circumspect was a waste of time for us both. 'I can smell it. The air's greasy with masala.'

'Jalfrezi,' she said, correcting me. I held her gaze. 'God you're fussy. Give me a moment.' She scuttled ahead, past racks of servers, turning right and out of sight. There came the noise of foil containers being crushed together.

Anyone who wanted to use the system could log in from elsewhere on site; there was no need to actually work in the lab. Still, Akshai was there all the time.

Most big companies I'd worked in had apocryphal stories of the individual living under their desk. In Akshai's case I suspected it could be true, although I'd never found evidence she was there for anything other than work.

Rhona asked me from time to time if Akshai had moved in, but that was as good as the story got.

By the time I reached the bank of screens set up in the heart of the Annexe she'd cleared away the worst of it and was wiping lurid rust coloured sauce from the table. The white surface had stained and her increasingly frantic rubbing wasn't making an impact.

'Leave it,' I said. 'Let's look at what's going wrong.'

We sat down together, our faces illuminated by screens of code staring down like distant stars brought close.

Two

I watched her work, remembered the feel of her skin against mine, her eyes drinking me in as we moved together. When I was with her I could push the outside world back beyond my trenches, force it to return to its side of no man's land for a few hours.

'The problem's here,' she said, unaware of my hungry gaze as she rolled across a section of data to enlarge it with a sweep of her hand.

'Don't tell me.' It's always easier to solve problems if you can spot them yourself, the context in which they're found offers clues to their undoing. The code was hers, elegant like her fingers; long, spare and beautiful.

The issue with elegant code is it can be so efficient that not everything being achieved by individual lines is obvious. Good code can be turned to direct many accomplishments at once. Good code is beautiful because it veers close to being beyond description.

Trying to explain it to Rhona the most helpful analogy I could come up with was to compare it to Da Vinci's *The Last Supper* within which is hidden a forty second composition you can only uncover by accepting that the bread rolls and the apostles' hands are notes across a musical staff.

An obvious problem sat on the screen before me like an angry cishet white male at a Pride parade. It wasn't immediately apparent what the section of code was supposed to be doing. I pointed at the key lines and murmured how it didn't seem right while I read the comments for clues as to its greater purpose.

Akshai smiled beside me. 'That's what I thought, too,' she said. 'But it's working fine.' She used one of the other screens to bring up the debugging tool which we used to trace its dependents; all those places into which it fed or which in turn relied on it in some manner. I tutted with the first blush of frustration, a feeling of stuttering pleasure which quickened the blood because we weren't dealing with something easy.

'So why show me that if it's not to blame?' I asked.

'I wanted to show this before I showed you the actual errors. I've run backwards through the code from the error and this is the place it breaks down. The code leading up to this point works fine.'

She flicked the object map onto the screen and highlighted the subsections, which were effectively borrowed from libraries people all around the world used and developed without thinking. We could therefore discard them as being the source of the problem.

I touched the back of her hand and she relinquished the touch pad, our gaze meeting for that sliver of time lovers grow into where understanding doesn't need words.

She showed me the spot in the output files where the error was logged. I squinted at the raw data, wishing she'd spent a few moments putting it into a format ordinary people could read.

'The entropy's negative.' I may as well have said time was running in reverse. 'This is clearly rubbish. Why'd you call me over something so obviously stupid?'

I could have been at the hospice, eating dinner and watching that ballroom dancing show with Rhona. Did I want to stay with Rhona? The thought just made me angrier because I knew the answer and it wasn't one I wanted to say even in the shuttered privacy of my own head.

We'd been sitting close but at my words Akshai shifted a little, her arms and thighs separated from mine by air where before they were resting together comfortably.

I wasn't in the mood for an argument. 'I don't have time for this. I didn't need to come in. You can manage it. You should manage it.'

'I didn't ask you to come,' she said quietly. I knew if I looked at her there'd be tightened eyes and teeth clamped together behind closed lips. She was patient with me, like a mother with a sick child.

Her care made me so angry.

'I've run it down,' she repeated, not letting me sink in the space between us. 'There's an ill-posed question which relies on some basic assumptions which, if varied, lead to huge changes in the solutions.'

Her words calmed me as if David were playing his psalms for a raging Saul.

'We built a series of transformations that should turn these solutions into a way of estimating the maximum likelihood but this…' She stopped, not knowing how to explain what we were looking at.

'This implies the black holes are distributing information as they evaporate.' I was missing something, like a monkey with its clenched hand trapped in a jar; the resolution sat with our own inability to let go of what we thought we knew. I was hers again with that simple conundrum, the howling in my chest dissipated as suddenly as it had come.

'They're creating information,' said Akshai.

An urge to dismiss the possibility sat on my tongue. I'd be saying what we both knew; if Akshai dared utter the same conclusion I'd castigate her for describing rather than explaining. The real question resolved in my head like a picture downloading slowly from the cloud.

'You called because you can't figure out why it's doing that.'

She shook her head, her fingertips lightly touching my arm to direct my attention back to the original piece of code.

'That's just it,' she pointed at the code. 'This is why it doesn't work.'

'You haven't changed this.' I spoke as much with hope as certainty. The entire simulation would have skittered off into gibberish if she had mucked around with it.

Akshai stood up. I caught a glancing blow of her scent; the same as Rhona's. When I first met Akshai it had been all I could do to hold back from asking her not to wear it. We'd only had the news a week or so when Akshai came for interview. Fortunately, I wasn't the only person assessing her because I could barely concentrate on what she was saying all the while she was in the room. Each time I took a breath Rhona would sear her presence across my mind, dates we'd been on, moments where I was nuzzled deep in her folds and all my world carried that smell.

I didn't remember the interview ending, nor if what I said in the debrief helped get her the job.

17

Now the wafts of her presence were my secret. Neither of them knew the other wore the same perfume.

We needed time to think.

'Rhona's got a new exhibition in mind.'

Akshai laced her fingers together in front of the blue corduroy skirt she wore. I didn't return the stare I could feel burrowing into my face.

'She'll need somewhere big. I was thinking of seeing if the company would sponsor it.'

'She won't like that,' said Akshai. 'She's never taken handouts.'

I wanted to ask her how she knew. Except she was right and if she knew it was because of all the times she'd listened to me talk about Rhona.

'Her idea is to play with perception, to ask us if what we see is really there or if it's something else. I thought we could tie it to encryption, maybe look at how that breaks what we know and leaves it there in front of us utterly incomprehensible without the right key.'

'Is that art?' she asked. Her face scrunched up trying to imagine it.

'I used to doubt her ideas,' I explained, remembering how I'd politely nod when Rhona excitedly outlined her latest concepts when I had the barest sense of what she was describing. 'Over the years I've grown to trust that when she's sure about something it'll work.' What more was there to say about my faith in her? Akshai stood quietly, wrestling with the notion. 'Her stuff sells for thousands,' I said, using an argument that would have left Rhona seething I was missing the whole point. Yet, in the end the rest of the world showed it believed in her through the frozen desire of money. What she and I thought didn't matter.

'When's she going to do it?' Her hand was rising to cover her mouth even as she spoke, trying to capture those traitorous words before they did their damage.

I torqued inside my head, nothing in focus while an answer, any answer, eluded me. Eventually, 'These things take her months to plan. She won't worry about the venue until she has the idea nailed down.'

For a while all we could hear was the hum and hiss of the servers and the air conditioning. It seemed darker to me, as if the lights had dimmed in response to our lack of movement.

'I want to change the code,' said Akshai. The strength of her conviction was undermined by how far she'd moved to say them, standing half hidden by the nearest rack of servers as if I might attack her for speaking.

The implications were mainly ones of inane frustration, of losing our time slot, of stopping the current round of simulations without any results. 'Who's lined up for time after us?' I asked, but I was already thinking through how long it would take to see if making the changes told us what was wrong with the code.

I brought up the resource queue for the servers to find it was empty.

'Who got fired?' It wasn't a serious question.

Akshai answered me with half a dozen different reasons, each was plausible but it hardly mattered which, if any, of them was right. What mattered was we had the entire server farm to ourselves for the evening.

She kept talking while I worked. The words didn't land but making sense of the world is who she is, it's how she controls all that space just beyond her body which doesn't succumb to equations or is too messy for logic to describe.

'You're up. Make me smarter and talk me through the changes as you do them.' Rhona's brother worked in finance and used the phrase whenever there was something interesting he didn't know but wanted to understand. It stuck with me for its efficiency and intent despite the fact it was corporate nonsense.

'We've been using Susskind's solution for conserving information as it crosses the event horizon.' She paused. 'Until today it was working fine. As the blackhole evaporated, the information emerging conformed to what we expected. Bits in, bits out. Now it's sending qubits to multiple recipients, so I'm going to delete your routine that articulates Strominger's Kerr/CFT correspondence for low angular momentum blackholes. That should force it into generating positive entropy.'

19

'Most of the community's suspicious about ASD/CFT correspondence anyway, because the real world doesn't scale uniformly,' I remarked, trying to remember when I'd written the code to which she was referring. So much of my time now was my own; Rhona's illness left me in a world whose legacies littered my life as the ruins of a fallen empire across an ancient landscape; great broken edifices, echoes of golden ages now past.

Ghosts everywhere wishing it was still their time.

'It's worked fine for us,' said Akshai without turning to look at me.

'I'm not criticising you; I was the one who wrote it. Won't it just bug out?' I couldn't see how removing a core piece of the mathematics would work. Algorithms are like recipes; miss out key ingredients and your cake is likely to come out of the oven tasting terrible.

She shook her head but didn't answer me. I could feel she was in flow so sat back, not wanting to disrupt her process. Once she'd fixed it she'd probably need some time to work out how to explain what she'd done. I certainly would if I were in her shoes. There were times when I'd solved particularly difficult problems and could only look at the screen marvelling at what I'd achieved. I could point out what I'd done, the actual lines I'd deleted, amended or written but couldn't explain, even to myself, how they integrated with the rest of the program to make it work. It often felt like I was grasping the memory of a precious dream which would greasily slip and slide out of sight if looked at directly. In the days after such events the wonder would fade as would my grasp of what I'd done, leaving me with an ashen sense that something had wanted to be uncovered and I was little more than its tool.

When I tried to explain this to Rhona she'd laughed, claiming I was an artist in the wrong profession. I couldn't see how the two were equivalent but it warmed me to think I wasn't so far away from the sculptor seeing the shape of what was waiting within an unhewn block of marble.

I left to go make a drink. Akshai liked hers as I did, black with half a sugar. I'd recently started drinking mine with a couple of drops of milk, like Rhona. It still made me grimace but I was growing to appreciate the way the milk tempered the cheap bitterness of our coffee.

The room was dark when I returned, the only light coming from the screens at which Akshai was working. As I walked through the room the overhead lighting came on but for a moment she was framed by the weak blue light of the screen, a lost soul flaring in the void.

Akshai took her coffee with both hands, sliding her chair back to let me in and kicking off the run as I sat down.

We waited while the program did its thing.

It took me a moment to understand what I was seeing when it came. The entropy was still negative. The blackholes were still creating new information.

'It's not even wrong,' said Akshai.

I could feel a pressure in my ears; if this was still wrong then what else was at fault in what we'd been doing? How far back did we have to go and how much of what we'd been doing was going into the bin?

'There's nothing wrong!' Burst out Akshai. She stood up, pushing her chair back as she bent over the desk, her face close to the screens.

'There clearly is,' I said. 'God damn it! Why didn't this come up before? What did you change?'

She twisted to face me looking panicked. 'Nothing. Literally nothing. I was simply running more of them than before. This is the largest exploration of information space we've run but all I did was change the parameters. The code allowed for that.' Her eyes were wide as she looked at me, defiant but pleading with me to believe her. 'I've not done anything.'

I scanned the results, parsing through the code, then switched back at Akshai. If she was right then months of work was in doubt. I felt like being sick.

I grabbed at one of the two keyboards, determined to stop the simulation from running on, ashamed someone might see the crap for which we were responsible. It didn't lift and my fingers slipped off without finding purchase.

Frowning, I tried again, but the keyboard didn't budge. I felt around the bottom for the gap with the desk but it was a smooth seam, as if both had been moulded from the same material.

'What is it?' asked Akshai, noting me scrabbling about.

'Something weird's going on.' I peered at the keyboard and watched as the keys melded together, the polymer taking on a glassy shine as it shifted under my gaze. Whipping my hands back and tucking them close against my body, I stood up, then crouched down to look under table but it was clear.

Akshai made a small sound, her throat constricting together in obvious fear. On the desk there was a mat of lichen-like material growing over the top of the keyboard, tendrils spiralling out across the desk. The lichen's pigments were hard to see, as if they were emitting in frequencies we couldn't process, playing at the edge of my vision as tiny gasps of light. Above it the images on the screens fractured into broken lines in myriad colours.

'We've broken it,' I said, a creeping sense of panic growing in my gut. What were we going to say to the company?

The screen went blank; then, with a blink of beige, numbers began scrolling from bottom to top like credits at the end of a movie. Most of them meant nothing to me but among them were the first ten digits of root two followed by the frequency of the hydrogen line.

'There's the left-handed chirality of a Dirac fermion,' whispered Akshai.

The digits of different universal constants stopped scrolling across the screens. At the tail end was a blinking cursor.

Three

Fundamental symbols of how the universe works sat before us, unwelcome graffiti on our computer screens. Ideas that had nothing, and everything, to do with simulating the evaporation of black holes over galactic time.

I didn't know what to do. 'Well.'

Akshai giggled, a high-pitched sound of fear bruised by the edge of hysteria.

It couldn't be someone trolling us; no one outside the company knew what we were doing, those who could understand it weren't many more. Nor was it an accident of the code – the results were too specific, too close to a textbook presentation of concepts that were invariant across physics.

A conversation I'd had with a mentor when I was still a post grad elbowed its way to the front of my mind but I wasn't willing to hear it out yet. Instead I avoided looking at the ossified keyboard and ran through other possible explanations. It couldn't be hackers because our staging environment was isolated from the cloud.

It could be a practical joke. I gulped with laughter at the idea even as I dismissed it; the keyboard sat on the desk demanding to know how anyone could change its very form. The world has no alchemists with access to the philosopher's stone.

'There is no philosopher's stone,' I muttered.

'If you were going to tell someone you were there, that's what you'd do,' said Akshai not listening to me as I wasn't listening to her.

We stared at the screens, stared at the mathematical spell writ across them like a sorcerer's handshake.

The cursor invited a response. Inside my head, my memory finally won out.

As an undergraduate I'd been taught quantum mechanics three times. Each time the material was presented using completely different representations so that each time we started anew it took several lessons to realise we were covering much the same content as we'd been taught the previous year.

The first time it made me swirl like a tree in a storm, angry but unable to do anything about it. However, by my final year I'd grown into myself sufficiently to approach my lecturer and ask why she was mixing up the subject again when most of us barely had a grasp from the last time they'd taken us through it.

'Because you weren't ready to learn it this way before,' she said as if I should be proud I was now deemed ready. 'When students first arrive all we can really do is start them on the basic ideas; we let those ideas settle in your minds and as you learn deeper concepts in other areas we bring you back to the subject and feed you more. At this point,' she meant the final semester of my degree, 'you're ready to learn the most elegant expression. It's the densest and most rewarding but that's exactly why you wouldn't have been ready earlier.'

'You could try us,' I countered, but she shook her head.

'We don't do these things on a whim. This approach comes from years of testing the most effective way of teaching these ideas.' She'd smiled at me. 'We all went through this. I remember half the battle was learning the new nomenclature, but later I realised that in the struggle I'd understood more about the ideas than from a perfect grasp of what I'd been shown the first time around.'

It felt to me like they were trying to be too smart.

'We're not trying to be cute,' she'd said, reading my expression, or as I realised later, benefitting from having had the conversation more than once. 'All that matters is we get you there. There's no point in being clever for our own sakes.'

'What about parity violations,' said Akshai, her fingers hovering over the keys of the panel as she calculated the best answer to give those on the other side of our screens.

'No. Fibonacci.'

She groaned. 'Sarah, that's such a cliché. We're not school kids.'

'That's the point,' I said. 'Any expansion will do, but anything more complicated and we have to start using symbols that people have made up to mean what we want them to mean. Will they understand ancient Greek?'

'We're really doing this?' She asked. I wondered if she was as clammy as I was. I surprised myself by just how calm I felt in the face of what we were facing; an alien race talking to us, as close as to be in the same room while being as far away as the most distant star.

I typed in 0, 1, 1, 2, 3, 5, 8, 13, 21, 34 and pressed enter.

The screens went blank, as if they'd been switched off. Cursing, we both ducked under the table to check cables but everything was still connected. The lights stayed on overhead, so it wasn't power we were lacking.

Emerging from under the desk, I saw the screens had returned to life. I stayed on my knees looking up, suddenly doubting everything which had happened in the last five minutes. Except the keyboard was still half organic, half glass.

A compulsion to tell Rhona everything gripped me by the throat. If she'd been there at that moment I would have told her about Akshai as well.

What I did know was I couldn't be there, not in that room, not with what was going on. Daylight wouldn't change anything; whoever was ruining my work would still be there, but I was tired and I'd promised Rhona I'd have breakfast with her before coming back to work.

'I'm going,' I announced to Akshai.

She stood up, moved to stand behind one of the chairs. 'What do we do about this?'

'It'll still be here in eight hours' time,' I said, almost believing it.

'I'm going to stay,' she said, hands gripping the chair like it might sublime if she didn't keep an eye on it.

Normally we would have kissed goodbye but I couldn't see her properly. She was distant, stood on land nearby in which a fissure had opened to separate us. I left, my head ducked low in case the world took firmer notice of us than it already had.

The house was dark, the air stale. Since Rhona had moved into the hospice the detritus of her illness had been cleared away to reveal my own tiny footprint; a dishwasher that took a week to fill, a bin that didn't need emptying and rooms into which no one went for days at a time.

Her piano sat covered, unplayed. The dregs of a forgotten coffee forgotten on the closed fallboard. Her slippers were quietly waiting under the stool for when she came home.

I wandered around the ground floor in a circuit from hall to kitchen to living room and back to the hall. I wanted to be at the hospice, telling Rhona what had happened, asking her what I should do.

She'd have no idea either but it didn't matter, it was the talking I needed. But it was too late; the hospice would be in darkness while its residents slept. Small humble lights would dot the night station and corridors as carers kept vigil but the peace there had a weight to it I hesitated to challenge.

I told myself Rhona wouldn't be sleeping. The pain was too much now, too ubiquitous, an ivy wrapped tightly around her trunk, its roots plunged into her bones.

I thought about SETI, about how many times I'd held court at dinner parties, announcing that we'd never find aliens out in space. I replayed boastful conversations in which I'd told people information was king, not energy, how intelligence would find us in information space not physical space. Besides, I'd utter, delivering the coup de grace, there's no different between the two.

Rhona would sigh and drink too much prosecco, but her cohort hung on the words of the one token scientist any of them knew.

Pulling into the car park at the hospice a little later, I refused to check the digital clock. As a relative I had a key to the building in which she slept, so I let myself in, feeling like I was trespassing on holy ground and expecting to be called to account at each step.

Her door was closed but soft light seeped from underneath. My heart raced at the hope she was awake. Looking up and down the corridor I slipped in, the handle like liquid in my fingers, slippery and firm at the same time.

Rhona's eyes were closed but she turned her head towards me as I shut the door.

'I'm sorry,' I started. 'Did I wake you?'

'What's happened?' She asked calmly.

The question wrapped around me like a warm welcome and I knew I was home.

I didn't know how to explain so started at the beginning, talking through what Akshai had done, about how we'd behaved as scientists do and changed just one variable to see what would happen. Except I had no words to convey the strangeness of the keyboard or how the screen had spewed universal constants with neither rhyme nor reason.

She waited patiently for me to get to the point and I felt how I would miss her more than I'd thought possible.

I watched her, taking in her face which was so withered from the illness that even her friends could no longer see in her the woman she was underneath its ravages. She lay waiting, her eyes closed and her breathing shallow while I grubbed around in the dirt of my mind for words to explain the fear I'd fled.

I didn't mention that Akshai was still there and the more I thought about it, the more I felt I'd done the wrong thing in leaving.

'Can you show me?' She asked.

'No,' I said, certain she shouldn't leave the hospice.

'What's the worst that can happen?' She asked.

There was no answer which didn't make me feel sick. 'I can't take you there,' I said.

To make up for my refusal I started talking about the search for alien life but didn't get far before Rhona laughed as hard as I'd seen her laugh for months before descending into a fit of ugly coughing. I filled a glass with water and fussed uselessly until she was released from its grasp. I was superfluous to her in those moments, with nothing to offer except patience while she suffered her body's ill temper.

'You found aliens?' She asked eventually, the broad smile still swiped across her face like a cat who'd got the cream. She didn't like me wiping spit from her chin, said it made her feel undignified so the glob hanging from her mouth took its own route down. I was past arguing about whether having drool untended to was undignified; it was what she wanted – some control over her life even if it was in the most ridiculous of things.

She listened to a halting explanation of what had happened, staring at me all the while with eyes still holding the vitality with which I'd fallen in love.

'I want to see it,' she said when my words ran out.

'We're not certain that's what it is,' I said. It was a weak reason not to take her but the strong reasons could stay away from us. Underneath my words was a fear the size of a tsunami of what might come through a door we'd opened without even knowing.

'You sound pretty certain from here,' she said. 'We've been together long enough for me to know when you're faking it, Sarah.' She shifted in the bed, struggling upright to face me more directly. 'Look at you, unable to sit still, fighting to find the words because you're so desperate to get the description right. That's the woman I love caring about what she's doing.'

'I can't take you from here; it's too risky. They'll come by to check on you and find you're gone. You know how cross they'll be.' I couldn't bear the thought of helping her from the bed, of smuggling her out of the hospice and hoping no one would miss her before I could get her back.

Rhona closed her eyes in a sign that she'd be crying if only her body was still able.

'I don't care,' she said quietly. 'It sounds fascinating, something I could use. I'm inspired, Sarah.' She looked at me, the candour in her eyes terrified me. 'I'm going to die.'

'You're going to be okay,' I interrupted. She waited for me to continue but there was nothing else to say.

'I'm going to die, my love. I want to see this before.' She stared right at me. 'Before that. We used to go on adventures. I never thought I'd find someone who wanted to see wonders with me but then you came along. My precious scientist.'

'An artist and a physicist walk into a bar,' I remembered how our friends described us. Recalling how we met.

'It wasn't my best work,' she said. 'I look back and find it hard to see what the Rhona who put that show together and I have in common.'

'I only went because I'd been challenged to see art as something valuable,' I sighed at how stand offish I'd been. 'I liked what I found.'

'Still punching above your weight?' She asked.

I took clothes from Rhona's wardrobe. Started to help her get dressed. 'You better believe it.' She couldn't leave in a dressing gown; a skirt and oversized sweatshirt would do. 'You're stuck with me, Ms Fisher.' She didn't have shoes any more, just slippers with woollen lining to keep her feet warm.

'Am I now, Ms Shannon?' Where did this joy come from? It didn't matter. What mattered was holding onto it for as long as it cared to visit.

Light rain pattered the outside door, forcing us to find an umbrella for the short walk to the car. I refused to let her get wet; that was a line I couldn't cross.

Rhona made me tell her the story again as we drove out of the hospice towards the company offices. It was easier the second time, easier with her by my side.

There was a plastic bag stuffed with her pills in the footwell, although I promised myself she'd be back by morning.

'I'm right, aren't I,' she said as we drove along empty roads, new LED street lights above, wet tarmac beneath.

'I'm glad you're here,' I replied. 'Do you think they'll ban me when they find out?'

She rasped out a laugh. 'Ban you from a hospice? For doing what the patient asked?' She set her face. 'Just let them try.'

The walk to the office was blustery, the rain heavier and coming in sideways making the umbrella pointless. I wrestled with it for about half the journey before giving up, folding it down and handing it to Rhona to use as a walking stick.

The lights in the building came on in response to us, shepherding our progress to our destination. We stopped at my office so Rhona could rest. We hadn't seen Akshai but I assumed she was still in the Annexe.

'Your keyboard looks normal,' Rhona said, disappointed.

'It's in the Annexe,' I replied. Then, seeing the sweat on her forehead I was struck with regret. 'Are you okay? We should get you back.' My phone showed we'd been gone nearly an hour. 'We can get you back before anyone notices.'

'I'm fine,' she whispered. 'C'mon, take me to see it.'

We walked together like an elderly couple through the corridor to the entrance where I buzzed us through.

'Sarah?' Came Akshai's nervous voice from inside.

'It's me,' I said, my heart jumping at her voice.

Akshai appeared between the servers, stopping mid-step when she saw Rhona. For her part I felt Rhona stiffen at my side. It wasn't how I'd envisaged them meeting; in fact I had never planned on them meeting. They'd become two separate worlds for me.

'Sarah told me what happened,' said Rhona. 'The woman I love has made contact with aliens and no damn cancer's going to stop me from seeing that.'

Akshai stood dumbfounded for a moment then said, 'I'll find another chair.' She dashed out of sight.

'She's not as pretty as I expected,' said Rhona.

'Why would you think she was pretty?' I asked without thinking.

Rhona didn't answer. Rather she stepped forward so I had to catch her up. I chided her for trying to do it without my help.

'I'm not a fucking child, Sarah.' She shook off my support, insisting she could manage the short walk on her own. We walked the rest of the way in silence.

Akshai dragged a casterless chair over to the bank of screens and fussed about Rhona until she was sitting comfortably.

Feeling the gooseberry, I reviewed what Akshai had been doing when we'd arrived.

'You're running the simulations?' I couldn't believe she'd been so reckless as to have tried it again on her own.

'I added back the code that was causing the errors,' she said. 'It's all working.'

'It's producing the same error as before?' I asked.

Ignoring me, she spoke to Rhona. 'How much did she tell you?'

Rhona blinked a couple of times then, deciding something I couldn't understand. She replied. 'Sarah told me the code was creating results you didn't expect.'

Rhona cut her eyes in my direction. 'Kind of. I decided to rerun the simulations as it was before, to see if I could replicate the problem.'

'But?'

'Nothing. The whole thing's running like it did yesterday. No errors, no problems, nothing like what happened.'

Rhona's fingers hovered over the lichen covered keyboard. 'Don't touch it!' I hissed, horrified she was even that close.

'I want to see what happened to make this,' she said. 'This didn't just happen out of thin air. You're the scientists, you know what you did. Show me.'

Part 2 – Isolation

Four

'The subroutines are back?' It was a stupid question to ask as Akshai had already told me.

She nodded, but within her small movement was a lie, peeking out from eyes which didn't rest on me except to glance away.

But lies deserve to be dragged out where they can be seen for what they are. 'What did you do?'

'Nothing. I was digging in the code after you'd left me.'

To the side Rhona stared at me, open eyed with surprise. The question she wanted to ask was clearly written upon her face; why had I left Akshai alone after what happened.

Akshai hadn't featured in my calculus at all, not until I'd changed my situation, not until I got to the hospice where I'd felt safe.

'Your routine had been reinstated by itself.' She took a breath and continued, her words tumbling out too quickly for interruptions. 'I didn't change anything, it was the same as when you arrived, before we made the changes to test the output. I've been up and down the code; nothing else has been altered.'

Rhona asked what that meant.

'I don't know,' said Akshai plainly. I saw then in the glued together eyelashes and puffy skin the evidence of tears.

How could I have left her alone? Instead of making sure she was okay I fled the lab hoping that anywhere else might be better than what we'd experienced. The lichen on the desk and keyboard had settled into a dusty grey, the quintessence which had energised it evanesced to nothing. Or perhaps just withdrawn.

'I'm sorry,' I said to Rhona. 'We don't know what's happened. None of this makes sense. It can't be what,' I stopped talking. Too embarrassed to say the word alien.

'So a magician came in and turned your keyboard to crystal via the medium of plant life?' Asked Rhona drily.

'It could have been hackers,' said Akshai, staring at her. I sometimes forgot how Rhona skewered bullshit wherever she saw it. She was a woman designed to keep me honest, connected to a world with which I'd have otherwise lost touch long ago.

'No it couldn't,' I said. 'Rhona's right.' I gestured at the keyboard. 'No trojan or exploit is going to alter reality, grow some moss and then tidily put our code back to what it was before we disturbed it.'

'So?' Asked Rhona, her eyes glittering as she watched me. I grew under her gaze, remembering how good we were together, how much sunshine had fallen on our lives, how much grace we'd had as friends and lovers.

Warily this time, whether cautious of the answer or Rhona I couldn't tell, Akshai asked, 'So what?'

'Do it again, obviously.'

Rhona sounded confident but I could see such boldness was wearing her out. It was a mistake to bring her to the lab. I had a sudden vision of her dying right there in her seat, leaving us a dead body to manage in the middle of the night.

Akshai was waiting for me to respond. Rhona had come to the lab to see what had happened, but her strategy, regardless of being driven by her own agenda, was sound.

'Akshai, if you're right then we should run the test again. Remove my subroutine and let's see what happens.' They were easy words to say, harder to turn into action.

When Akshai didn't start resetting the software I gently pushed my chair between her and Rhona to do it myself. She let her chair roll back enough to give me space.

I tried not to think about having Rhona on one side and Akshai on the other.

It took a few minutes to make the change and recompile the code. In my head it felt like seconds.

'I guess I better run it this time,' I said, trying to lighten the mood.

They waited for me to get on with it.

The code began running, the simulations cranked up and data was crunched.

We were back at the bottom of the mountain, the sky further away than we'd thought.

'When does it happen?' Asked Rhona.

'It's not,' said Akshai. 'It had already happened by now. Last time.' She tapped on the keys, scrolling up and down through the program as it ran. Rhona started to cough, the dry hollow sound echoing around the room and drowning out the hum of the servers.

'This was a mistake,' I announced. 'God, what was I thinking?' I stood up to help Rhona from her chair. We could be back at the hospice by three and with a huge amount of luck no one would have noticed her absence. I was angry, with what I didn't know, but all that mattered was getting Rhona home and safe again.

They both spoke at the same time.

'Sarah,' called Akshai.

'Is it supposed to be doing that?' Asked Rhona.

I froze, my route back to normality slamming shut in those two sentences.

The bank of screens was full of equations. Not numbers this time but maths proper – the language of the universe itself, as heedless of actual numbers in the same way as French or Japanese.

They scrolled across the screen too quickly for me to follow but whoever was putting them there had learnt their Greek, their nomenclature, and was painting integration signs, equations of state, triple parenthesis conditional statements as they went. It was beautiful to me, my own Greyson Perry.

In some parts it was more logic than mathematics, statements about the difference between domains and ranges, real, imaginary and irrational. The hard, sparse script slithered across the screen, giving way to arcs and diagrams that appeared to have been drawn freehand, the background colours turning from black to tan then cream.

'It's beautiful,' said Rhona. I held her hand and for a moment we watched something surpass our understanding, united by our awe.

'This is different,' I said, meaning seeping into my consciousness. It was more than before, deeper, and it was already longer than the previous event. Beside me Akshai was filming with her phone, hardly paying attention to what was happening as she tried to capture it.

One of screens blinked, then an image of the lichen appeared at the centre, a small tenticular blob of growth around delicate central platelets, shown within the picture rather than there on top. I stepped back, unnerved, and pulled Rhona's seat back as I moved.

Within the screen the lichen grew, its arms whirling as a spiral galaxy in miniature. It pressed up against the edge of the screen while equations describing the grounding of the universe continued to etch themselves across the rest of the monitors.

For a time the image squidged within the confines of the screen, the arms curling around and distorting its shape until there was nothing to see except a picture of a squashed plant with only the tiniest gaps showing the cream background.

The formulae being presented to us were no longer recognisable. Occasionally familiar elements could be picked out but the symbols were being used in ways I didn't understand in fields I couldn't identify. It wasn't that they were growing more complicated or lengthy, just the opposite, they were increasingly simple, elegantly Spartan. There was the possibility we were being shown nonsense but in my gut I was certain they represented the world in ways which no one on Earth had yet conceived.

'There's a dozen Nobel prizes in there,' I said to Akshai, pointing her away from the lichen to focus on the text. She shifted the phone a few degrees, stepping back to join us and in so doing taking in the entire bank.

'Will your resolution be good enough?' Asked Rhona. 'I tried this for an exhibition and the fidelity wasn't up to it.'

Akshai lowered the phone. 'I can zoom in right?'

'That's the problem,' said Rhona. 'It looks terrible. If you want to see those equations later you need to be sure that being so far away is ok.'

I pulled my own phone out and began filming. 'Akshai, Check it. Check the recording. I'll film while you do it.'

'Spit,' said Akshai after reviewing the footage. 'It's okay until I stepped back.'

'I'll film for now.' I was closer than her, having drifted in unconsciously while waiting for her to check.

The equations stopped scrolling across the screens, coming to a halt as if whoever was writing them had grown tired of putting them up for us to see. Unlike the previous time there was no cursor for us to write a response.

The image of the lichen pulsed, the centre of it bulging in the one, two rhythm of a heartbeat. The arms unspooled, spilling onto the thin black frame of the screen like a sleeper stretching upon waking. The sound of chairs scraping against the floor filled the room and suddenly Akshai and I were further away from the desk. Rhona's chair didn't move so easily and I rushed back to pull it to safety.

The tendrils pulled away from the screen, waving around in space seeking purchase on another surface. From the thicker limbs tissue thin threads wafted into the air like those silken lines spiders ride on a summer's day.

One of them touched the surface of the desk, away from the ossified keyboard. Immediately the nearest tendril swung down, following its line, extending its tip until it too landed on the desk. Like ivy it placed adventitious roots shaped as tiny little toes as anchors then throbbed, light spilling from its length across the entire spectrum with a soft glow concentrated in veins that had been invisible before that moment.

Rhona sat still, watching the lichen grow out from the point where it touched the desk, repeating the same pattern as before; a central node from which arms curved out in five directions.

Akshai circled around us, filming. My own camera hung uselessly in slack arms, filming nothing but the floor. I pulled it up to cover the desk, scanning vertically to the screen from where other arms continued to search for their own destination.

'We've got to leave,' said Akshai. She stood off to my right, level with the screen but facing its side. Leaving Rhona in the chair, I joined Akshai and found I'd forgotten how to breathe. From the back of the screen dozens of tendrils stretched in the same way the roots of the banyan tree reached out; intermingled, straight, multitudinous.

39

They weren't moving as those emerging from the screen did. Instead they grew as we watched them, like sugar cane or bamboo which can almost be heard groaning as they grow inches in a single day. They stuck straight out from the back; at some point they'd collapse under their own weight.

'Sarah,' said Rhona, her voice weak, shot through with broken chords.

I turned to find a tendril between us, slowly dancing as it sought out somewhere to place its roots. Rhona wasn't looking at that; her eyes were fixed on another that was waving inches from her legs.

There was no way for her to get out of the chair without touching the intruder. The desk was covered in lichen, the spirals, hairy with small thin sprouts of their own spread across the surface, hugging it as they wrapped tightly around the underside.

The colour they gave off didn't illuminate, rather it highlighted just how alien it was, reminding me of the small fireflies you could find in the woods at night just outside of the city that would blink slowly in the darkness, pinpricks of unexpected life.

'Sarah,' said Rhona again. Akshai had troubles of her own as the single tendril that had precipitated out of the air on her side split into two, both of which blocked her immediate route out of the room.

I watched the waving between us, saw how it was describing regular if increasing circles and ducked under to reach Rhona. I ran around the back of her chair and pulled her out of the way.

'Are you okay?'

'Thank you,' she said. 'This is a bit closer to it than I'd anticipated. I didn't know *what* I was expecting.'

The scientist within me could see her only as a liability, a weakness we had to account for that sucked valuable brain power away from dealing with what we'd unleashed in the company's single most expensive lab filled with their unique cutting edge quasi-quantum computing network.

The other me saw her fear and wanted to pick her up and leave, to take her somewhere safe from this and hold on tight.

'We can't just leave,' I said to Akshai with my hands on the back of Rhona's chair. 'If this stuff touches the servers the whole place could get corrupted.'

The desk was two metres clear of the nearest racks on all sides but the tendrils were half that length already and displayed behavioural signs that made my throat tighten. I realised that none of them were questing downwards in the wake of the first of them touching the desk. Each of the remaining tendrils fanned out sideways; hovering in the air as best they could, they searched through the volume of space around them.

The desk was covered now apart from the corner farthest from the two keyboards. The growth had piled up on the electronic equipment, sending shoots along the length of the cables that hung off the desk and disappeared into the raised floor upon which we stood.

'They're following the electric fields,' I said, understanding suddenly how they were navigating.

'If we switch off the power they'll have nothing to look for,' said Akshai.

'We don't know how much energy they need to grow like this,' I responded. My comment was stating an unknown – neither of us knew if thinking about it would help or hinder us from making the right decision.

'Can't you just switch everything off?' Asked Rhona.

'No,' said Akshai as I said 'Yes.'

'The backup generator will come online within a fraction of a second and the system will switch over to the alternate grid feed automatically,' said Akshai, reciting facts I knew as well as she did.

'It's built to withstand multiple points of failure. They call it two N plus one resiliency,' I said, thinking through what she was saying. 'The entire site's designed to keep the power running even if the world outside falls to pieces. The generator can go for eight hours without needing more diesel.'

'So, what then?' said Rhona.

'I don't know,' I hissed. 'Let me think.' Rhona closed her eyes at my temper. I wanted to apologise but her gabbling was the distraction that kept me from thinking.

'What about the extinguishers?' Asked Akshai.

I thought through the different types that we had available. 'Nothing's going to help. We can't set it on fire – simply too much energy. We can't cool it down and what good's it going to do covering it in non-conductive powder?' I stared at the servers as if inspiration might come jumping out from their blinking facades.

'Pull the plugs out,' said Rhona. My irritation at the sound of her voice turned to joy when I processed what she was saying.

Akshai was ahead of me, having already turned to tackle the nearest server. I ran to those on my left, fumbling in my pocket for the keys that allowed us access to the cages. It took us several minutes to get into and unplug the ring immediately surrounding the desk. It wasn't enough to disrupt the simulation whose code had been developed to scale with the number of available processing cores.

'We need to stop the simulation,' I shouted across the hall.

'Do you know which server is the head?' Akshai shouted back. I had no idea. On the other side of the room I could hear Rhona coughing.

We came back into the space around the desk. The tendrils were longer now on Akshai's side, the two having split into four. On my side, which was closer to the limb of lichen that had grown over the desk and down into the floor underneath us, the tendril had remained singular, swaying gently as it extended towards the first rack of disconnected servers.

'I can't get out,' said Akshai. 'The roots on the back block my path that way and these,' she pointed at the four tendrils reaching for her servers. 'There're too many of them.'

'Jump over them,' I said, meaning those that had grown out of the back of the screen. Akshai nodded and moved to leap over the coil of black roots just behind the desk.

I heard a weak moan from behind me and turned to see the lichen had spread onto the floor from the desk and was touching the leg of Rhona's chair.

Spit ran down her mouth and her skin was pale. I realised she wasn't conscious. I ducked under the nearest tendril, felt it touch my jumper as I passed, and ran for Rhona.

The lichen beat me to her, its swirling light touching her foot as I got there.

Five

Rhona's backed arched in a grotesque parody of pleasure, her chin reaching for the ceiling as eyes opened and mouth gaped. My fingers reached for her but refused to connect. Instead I crouched down, a scream of denial escaping my lips. Where was Akshai? Why wasn't she helping me?

Then, like a woman waking from a coma, Rhona took a long rasping breath that broke into juddering gulps so deep I prayed for her to exhale. The lichen etched itself across her foot, an infection taking root. Its colours grew deeper, cerulean then a deep rich scarlet all the while glowing from within. Crushing my fear with shame at not having already acted, I grabbed the heel of her slipper and pulled it into the air. The strands of lichen stretched and broke away like molten cheese, severing its connection with the tendril that had crawled across both the floor and then the chair to reach her.

Flinging the slipper to the side my heart screeched when I saw spores blooming on her bare feet. I blinked away tears but couldn't shake the tightness in my body as I tried to think of something, anything I could do. I would have torn down the world to change what was happening to Rhona.

A soft movement of air by my ear caused me to flinch. Turning to see what it was I fell backwards, scrabbling to avoid the tendril that had been reaching for her face as it swung fractions of an inch past my head.

'We've got to get out of here,' shouted Akshai. She'd found her way around the server room and was standing in the route between the servers that led to the Annexe's exit. It was as if she stood alone on the dance floor of a nightclub, lights strobing across her as she waited for us.

'I can't.' My words choked in my mouth. 'I can't leave Rhona.' Her body was frozen in position, her face staring, unseeing, at the ceiling. Her hands clenched the chair, taut and pincerlike, the fingertips digging into the armrests so hard her nails were bent backwards.

Words escaped my lips but I couldn't tell what I was saying. All that mattered was to get Rhona out of the Annexe and away from what was happening.

A smell like salted popcorn made my stomach growl. I turned to see what could be making it but there was no obvious origin for an aroma so strong it was now closer to burnt butter. The tendril near to Rhona pushed forward, sensing that she was close, that its kin had already found her and she was their true target.

I pulled on her arms, trying to get my hands underneath so I could lift her. The illness had emptied her out, hollowed her bones and shrunk her organs. Before it she had weighed more than I did so now I believed, had to believe, that she was light enough for me to carry on my own.

Except I couldn't get her moving. Teardrops splashed onto her hands as I yanked, careless of the damage I might do to her; I had to move her, I had to save her.

'Sarah, you have to get out,' said Akshai.

I ignored her. How could she want me to go with her now? How could she want me to leave Rhona behind just when she needed me the most?

Tendrils burst from her foot, pushing out without damaging the skin, as if they were part and parcel of one another, as if Kafka had written his story just about her.

A sob bubbled between my teeth and for a moment I couldn't see anything as my eyes squeezed shut.

No. I wouldn't leave her. I pulled again on her hand and felt her wrist dislocate with a click and a pop, coming away from the chair at an angle while her arm remained glued to it. Screaming, I dropped her hand, saw it lay there hanging off the side of the armrest without so much as a twitch. I heard someone say, 'No, No! No, no, no *no!*' And realised it was me.

'It's reaching for you too!' Shouted Akshai, sounding desperate.

'Go,' I called back. 'Call the company. Tell them what's happened. They have to help us.'

'What am I going to say?' She called back. I understood she didn't want to leave me there alone, that she was as frightened as I was.

Except we weren't the same; I was frightened not for myself but for Rhona and in that moment I realised Akshai was frightened for me. We were heads each looking at different people, unable to see those looking at us in turn.

'Tell them it's a nine on the Rio scale.' I didn't have any more words for her and stopped looking to see if she'd gone.

'I'm sorry, my love,' I started. 'I can't help you. I can't do anything. I would. You know that. And I'm sorry. I shouldn't have brought you. I didn't have to bring you. God, why is this happening?'

The roots protruding from her foot sank onto the ground, throwing out anchors to fix her in place. The untethered tendrils growing from the screen continued to multiply and a disproportionate number of them twisted in Rhona's direction.

'I'm going to have to go. Hold on until I can come back. Promise you'll wait for me.' The tears rolled down my cheeks. The thought that I deserved this scraped through my head, a knife inside a scallop shell, removing any sense of action as it travelled from the front to the back of my mind. I squeezed her arm as tightly as I dared and crawled on my backside towards the exit, keeping her in sight the whole way.

As if waiting for me to get out of the way the tendril that had been by my head plunged into her chest followed by another that touched down on her arm and then a third that nestled gently in her hair.

I curled up by the door unable to stand.

Time passed.

I levered myself up with my back to the exit to see what had happened. Where she'd been sitting was covered in branches and arms of lichen as thick as my arm, sulphuric yellow edges around royal blue channels of light. Underneath it somewhere lay Rhona, but she was completely buried. From there the lichen was spreading out, inches per second in all directions. It had found and overwhelmed the first ring of servers around the desk, climbing over them as if they were logs fallen in the forest laying between it and the real quarry.

The door pushed against my back. I crawled out of the way to find Akshai standing over me. Without hesitating she bent down and pulled me up to my feet. With one arm under mine, she led me out of the Annexe and into the adjoining corridor.

The door pulled shut of its own accord, closing with a puff of pressurisation from within the server hall.

'Did you call them?' I asked, staring at the door.

'There wasn't anyone there,' she said. 'I sent an email.'

I laughed then, pressure bursting up from within; Rhona was on the other side of the door. Beyond my help, going through something I couldn't imagine and all we'd managed to do was send an email.

'I've got the director's personal number.' The words were my thoughts as they came, the idea unmediated by consciousness.

Akshai walked with me back to my office.

The lights were flat and warm, bland compared to what had grown from our screens in the Annexe. It seemed to me that we were standing in a poor copy of the real world whose creators weren't interested in fostering a sense of immersion but wanted us to accept that the desk, the picture of Rhona, the cards left over long from my birthday, that all of it was there to fill in the background and nothing more.

I stood against this scene, not within it, not as a part of it. I felt the same as I did on the day Rhona had been diagnosed.

On autopilot I dialled the director.

'Sarah? What's wrong?' Her voice had the blurred edge of the just awoken.

I told her what had happened. Kept restarting, saying 'let me take a step back.' To her credit she listened in silence and didn't hurry me along at any point.

At the end of it she asked, 'Where's Rhona now?'

It wasn't the question I was expecting; nothing about the phenomena we'd fled, nothing about the messages on the screens.

'She's still in the Annexe,' I said as my confession, holding back a complete disintegration at the sound of the words in my ears. 'I left her behind.'

'Sarah. Listen to me very carefully. You did the right thing. You're going to feel this was your fault, but it isn't. You were doing something kind, something beautiful for her. Don't hold onto this as being laid at your door.'

Except I'd brought her to the lab. I'd taken her from the place where she was safe. If Rhona hadn't come she'd still be okay. And she only came because I made it possible.

The director was still speaking. I put her onto speaker so Akshai could hear too.

'What's important now is to isolate the lab and ensure that nothing escapes. We have no idea what you've encountered, nor what it wants. If this truly is a first contact event then there are protocols we've agreed as a board. I need to get onto to that. God help us get this right.'

Her confidence soothed me and the world came into focus, pulled me into it so that I belonged again. I sat in my office and everything was real because we had hope that we could make things right.

'What about us?' I asked.

'Stay there. It hasn't moved out of the Annexe but we need people on the ground to observe until others can arrive and take over.'

'We tried isolating the system,' said Akshai.

'You unplugged the servers nearest the eruption point. I understand. But the facility is still running. There's little we can do about that right now. I can't activate a shut down without board approval and that won't come until we've met.' She paused. Akshai and I exchanged glances, waiting on her together. Her voice faded as she turned her head away from the speaker, acting even as she continued to talk to us. 'You can monitor the system from your office. Observe and let me know if anything changes. People will start arriving on site in about thirty minutes. After that it's going to get crazy, so take some time now to breathe deeply. You're going to be telling your story a great many times in the next few hours and I

47

want you to know what it is you're saying because any detail you miss, any element you elide or pass over might be the critical one in getting Rhona back and containing this.'

Akshai reached out and took my hand with the softest of squeezes.

'Sarah. We will do everything we can to get Rhona back for you. Please, don't worry, she's at the top of my priorities. In what happens next I need you to remember that because it's going to seem like no one cares for her the way you do. Can you remember that for me?'

At any other time I would have bristled at being spoken to like a child but her words were a life raft to stop me from drowning in the storm.

'Thank you,' I said.

The director hung up. In the silence of the severed line Akshai moved in and held me while I cried for Rhona.

I watched Akshai's face, open and beautiful, her angular cheekbones highlighting eyes large enough to drink me in. Underneath her right eye were a triangular trio of small moles I called 'my therefores'. They were the first place I ever kissed her. We'd been sitting in her small messy flat after drinks straight from work. She'd approached getting to know me sideways, knowing I was with Rhona, knowing that she was sick. Akshai never offered herself as a replacement. Instead I found somewhere I could hide, a space I could escape the pit in which I'd come to live while Rhona deteriorated regardless of each promising new treatment the doctors tried.

'I'm sorry, Sarah,' said Akshai, stirring me out of my own introspection.

'You don't have to be sorry,' I said, not following why she was apologising.

'I couldn't get to you. I tried but that thing was in the way.'

How she'd managed to get out without getting infected as well I didn't understand. Smiling at her in what I hoped was more than a thin bleak arrangement of my mouth I said, 'It's okay.' But it wasn't.

My desktop pinged, indicating activity in the Annexe. We both perked up, swinging our attention to the computer. There was no camera in the linking corridor but the ping told us that the door had been opened from the inside.

'What do we do?' Asked Akshai.

'We've got to go look,' I said. Not feeling at all certain that we should.

'We can stay at the other end of the corridor,' she said, making it sound like that short stretch of carpet tiled sterility was a buffer the other side would respect. 'Wait here. I'll be right back.'

She returned to find me hovering by the door to the office, head cocked to one side so I could look down the hall for her return. She'd found a large torch that appeared reassuringly heavy. I didn't think it was going to be any use but somehow it made me feel better.

We pushed open the double doors to the connecting corridor to find the lights were off. They didn't come on at our arrival as they were supposed to.

'Who would have thought you'd be using that for its actual purpose?' I asked her.

Akshai shone the beam in the distance.

'Sarah?' Asked a voice from the Annexe.

It was Rhona's voice but not quite, as if she were speaking as part of a harmony, hers only one identity among many others. The edges of her tone were bounded with deep timbre and falsetto, stretched wider than her natural range.

'I'm here,' I said. Akshai reached out to hold me back from running down the corridor.

The beam of light found Rhona; she was standing on the threshold, lichen around her feet and growing up her legs. Her clothes had been replaced by the growth, the shape of her body muted, diluted so it was impossible to tell if she still had legs under the spreading platelets of yellow and blue.

Her head was her own, her skin glowing with rivulets of green light that shone from under the surface.

When I looked into her eyes I saw nothing of the woman I loved.

'Are you okay?' I asked.

'She is here, inside, there but so are I, they, we,' she said to me.

'What have you done?' I said. I wanted to dash at her, to pull the growth from her body, to free her from whoever they were.

A stream of meaningless syllables spilled out in answer, a word salad that meant nothing to us. It continued without a break and after a while each new phrase hit me in the throat as I realised she wasn't there at all.

Then English again. 'It's taken us, I, them some time to parse your symbols. We, they, you will continue to make mistakes. Do you understand?'

'Don't stop talking,' I said. Beside me, Akshai held the torch steady the beam reflecting from the cat's eye of her skin.

'This is your form? We, us, I find it important to present us, we, all in a way you will understand. She is here, there, inside. She will blur who, what, how we are here, there, with you. It cannot be permanent, eternal but only now, temporary, gone.'

'Will you give her back to me? Please, give her back to me.'

'We, they, all do not understand your actualisation but she is not working in a way biology would predict, trajectory, evolve. She, I, we like playing the piano.' She frowned and it was the first expression her face had shown.

'She's sick,' I said. 'She's all I've got. Please give her back to me.'

Rhona didn't answer. We heard voices calling from inside the main facility. I took my eyes from Rhona for a moment, just a fraction of a second but when I turned back she was gone and the door to the Annexe was shut.

'Rhona!'

The door behind us opened. 'Please, step back. Are you okay?' I nodded dumbly as bright lights were shone in my face.

Someone said, 'I need you to come with us. We're going to make sure everything's okay.'

Hands took a gentle hold of my arms and my shoulders. So many people were all around us. Akshai was led away, we parted without saying goodbye and suddenly, among those newcomers on all sides, I was alone.

Six

Decontamination. A washing away of corruption, a cleansing of pathogens and a way of keeping others safe.

The hands that led us away from the corridor to the Annexe took us out of the building, Akshai in one direction, me in another. White and blue suits made from air tight fabric with helmets covering their entire faces as if we were survivors of a picnic in Pripyat and they our rescuers.

After being asked if I was okay no one else spoke until we reached a small tent outside the main facility. Harsh halogens turned night into day and the blue canvas skin of the tent bleached white on the inside from their power.

Within the tent, which was thirty-six feet by twenty four, were beds, steel tables partially dressed in white sheets for people to lie on, together with cabinets and fridges. I was shown to a corner and told to wait.

Around me people moved with purpose, conversations held about me as if I wasn't there.

A hazmat suit with a woman's face showing through the Perspex panel approached.

'Follow me. We're going to get you cleaned up.'

It was news that I needed cleaning but then whoever the company had brought in wasn't taking chances; there was nothing here in the facility that was considered biologically dangerous but they moved with the grace of those for whom this was a well-practised dance. Each and every partner knew their role, their positions and their cues and I a particle of smoke in their midst.

She walked me to a small doorway and waited until I realised she wanted me to go ahead of her. I stepped into a small cubicle where a disembodied voice told me to undress and move into the decontaminant shower in the next chamber.

There was nowhere to hang my clothes.

'We'll look after your clothes. There will be fresh garments when you're finished here.'

So I did as I was told. It might have been early September but the night was chill and, shivering, I entered the shower hoping that at least the water would be warm.

Which it wasn't. The more awake, rational me might have considered where they were going to get hot water so rapidly but it was late and I was exhausted. I stood there, arms across my chest, unable to even dance as jets of icy spray hit me from all sides.

'Raise your arms, please. Turn around slowly.'

I did as I was told, the cold water speckling me with countless tiny pricks of pain. The shower ended and my hands dropped to my side. Before I could open my eyes a puff of powder hit my head, followed swiftly by half a dozen other thwops as small pellets burst their contents onto my skin. Then the water started up again and I could feel the dust frothing, tingling as it scoured my skin for whatever it was they were worried about.

I reasoned they couldn't know about the lichen or they'd not have bothered with the decontamination process.

The water stopped a second time and it was over. I opened my eyes, my skin pimpled with the cold. A young African woman dressed in plain blue military fatigues handed me a huge, soft towel.

'C'mon,' she said in a strong rounded Birmingham accent. 'We can't have you catching your death after all that's happened.'

Into yet another room, as if rather than tents they'd erected a maze through which I was slowly being led like a rat while they watched my progress from above.

At least it was furnished. Tables, chairs, the smell of coffee machines working overtime. A tray of croissants, pastries and unripe bananas. To the side a bundle of clothes: a fitted white t-shirt, ocean grey, loose-fitting sweat top and trousers together with toneless underwear and a pair of black plastic sandals.

'What will you drink?' She asked me while I dressed.

I took a mug of coffee and a banana, my stomach growling at the smell and reminding me that dinner had been instant soup downed before I'd gone to the hospice the first time more than ten hours earlier.

Oh god. They'd be going spare over Rhona by now. My phone had disappeared along with my clothes and I feared the number of missed calls, the likelihood they'd already called the police.

We sat at the table. 'We've got a few minutes,' she said.

'Where's Akshai?' I asked. I didn't know if I should be worried that she hadn't joined me.

'We need to process you separately,' said my host. Holding out a hand to be shaken she said, 'I'm Adeola.'

'Sarah.'

'Sarah Shannon,' she said, confirming that they knew who I was already. 'It's nice to meet you. I know you have lots of questions and before the interviews start I'm here to try to answer as many of them as can be answered.' Before I could open my mouth she held up a hand. 'There's going to be a bunch of things I can't answer – best we talk about those first.' She counted them off on her fingers as if they were items on a shopping list she didn't want to forget. 'We work for the company, as do you, but I can't tell you any more than that. I can't say when the process will be over – if you answer everything a dozen times precisely the same way they might conclude that they've got what you know,' she smiled sympathetically. 'You won't see your colleague again until this is all over, as she'll be undergoing an identical process. At the end of this you'll have to sign rather strict nondisclosure forms. Lastly, I'm pleased to say that you'll be expected to take some time off before returning to work. The company's genuinely delighted to have you on the team and wants to make sure you're okay before you do anything so stressful as come back into the office.'

'My wife is in the Annexe,' I said.

Adeola frowned, touched her ear and listened for a moment. When she was done she fixed me with a direct stare. 'There's no one in the Annexe. We've got thermal imaging cameras set up and we can only identify the servers you didn't unplug.'

'What about the lichen?' I asked.

'Whatever else is in there isn't giving off a heat signature.'

53

"Don't be ridiculous. Even stone has an ambient temperature, it's that scale from cool to hot that makes for the spectrum.'

'You'd think so,' she said agreeably. 'Except we can see the room as it's supposed to be but that's it for the moment. If there's anything else in there we're not seeing it, which includes Ms Fisher.'

'But we left Rhona in there.'

'I can't say what's happened to her.' She glanced upwards as she listened to her own words. 'What I mean is that we can't say because we don't know. If she was in there, she's not there now. The imaging gives us a complete view of what's there, it's builds up a fully three dimensional picture of the room.'

'But you're going to get her back.' It wasn't a question. I couldn't let it be a question. 'The director said it was her top priority.'

Adeola fixed me with an open-eyed stare. 'We are doing everything we can to find her.'

'Can you at least see the lichen?' I asked, feeling defeated.

'This is really a question for your debrief. I'm best able to answer questions about what's happening on the more practical side of things.'

The director's advice played in my ears along with Adeola's deft changing of the subject. 'How many of you are here?' I asked.

'Enough,' she said, another dead end. 'An army,' she conceded. 'All of this needs a lot of people.'

'What happens now?'

'Well, after we're done you'll be debriefed, which is far less glamorous than it sounds.'

'It doesn't sound in any way glamorous.'

She showed me a wry grin, 'then you've got an inkling of just how detailed it's going to be. Once that's done? I can't say. It all depends on what happens in there and if this is a real Rio Scale event.'

'If it's not?' I asked, not really sure why I cared.

She shrugged. 'We all go home and you get the dismal job of explaining how you ruined months of work and millions in funding. I'm sure that's not where we're going, though.'

I wasn't convinced she believed what she'd been told. Perhaps they'd given her nothing on which to hang her hat, perhaps they'd instructed her to mind me while they figured out what was going on. The company had projects all around the world which I knew were as cutting edge as mine but we didn't meet each other outside of conferences; we were expensively maintained and determinedly kept apart in case we contaminated one another.

'Have you got negotiators here?'

'Another one for the proper debriefing,' she wagged her finger at the table between us. 'Why don't I try to tell you what you need to know.'

I looked away, submitting. I didn't think she had anything I wanted to hear.

'We're the rapid response team. Our job is to isolate the site, quarantine it. You and your colleague Ms. Slim were here when the event was called in, so we treat this like we would a biohazard incident. You've both been decontaminated, you'll both be debriefed. Given the nature of the situation specialists will be on their way to address the more... esoteric... elements in play. More mundanely, we'll feed and clothe you, communicate with the authorities as required, make sure you get some sleep and do our best to ensure that nothing here spills into the outside world. I would love to be able to say that your life won't change, that everything can go back to how it was but I can't.' She looked at her watch then back at me. 'Life has consequences, Ms. Shannon. We can't run the clock back and start over, but we'll do our best to make tomorrow seem like yesterday.'

'What about Rhona.'

'If Rhona is here then we'll find her.'

I started to protest that Rhona was in the Annexe when the lights above us flickered.

'Generator's probably not been set up properly,' said Adeola. 'We bring our own power supply in case we can't rely on the local grid.'

Then it went dark. Inside the tent it was pitch black, the kind of darkness where you can feel your hand in front of your face but truly can't see it there.

'Stay here,' said Adeola. I heard her stand up and leave, slowly feeling her way out of the room. Without the hum of the generator and the distraction of our conversation I could hear others moving about. People were shouting, running, there was every element of human beings panicking.

All that separated me from the rest of the world was a few millimetres of canvas. A huge bang sounded from the facility, a shock of shattered glass followed by silence into which the cries of the wounded could be heard.

There was no way I was staying inside the tent. Using my hands to lead me I emerged into the outside, feet on grass and no one nearby to stop me. The facility was at the edge of a massive low rise high-end office park just off a motorway junction and landscaped with lakes, woodland and trails that gave each of the individual blocks the illusion of seclusion.

The company had set up its incident unit between the main building and the lake separating it from the next block along, which belonged to a global pharma corporation who, despite having let the building three years ago, let it lie empty.

There were a half dozen of these giant tents, although not all of them were finished. Whatever was going on had drawn everyone away from the site and into the facility. The power was out across the building but the glow of street lights from the road let me pick my way across the grass towards the Annexe.

Before I got there people came running out in the opposite direction. Some were dressed in military clothing while others wore the hazmat suits I'd been greeted with earlier. Regardless of their gear they were united in their flight. Gaping holes scarred the facility where before there had been glazing, staring back at me as a broken mouthed grin from which glinted the fractured white light of the street.

The first few people ran past without stopping but the remainder slowed up, drawing to a halt beside me as I watched the building from which they'd fled. Crooked limbs of lichen grew across the outside of the Annexe in a thin caul riven with thicker veins that pulsed a deep crimson like cooling lava.

A hand on my arm urged me to step back but I shook it off. What had they done in there? Was it the intruder exerting itself, engaging in a second expansion now it had control of the facility? Why had the windows blown out?

I moved closer even as others continued in the opposite direction. Rhona was there.

I got to concrete under foot. Glass chips crunched as I walked and the curl of dying flames could be seen from inside the building. Emergency fire doors were flung open, hanging wide as an invitation to the reckless, and then I was inside.

Green-white fire lights illuminated doorways, fluorescing beaded runways on the floor mapping out clear routes through the building which I followed in reverse, deeper into the hungry darkness towards the Annexe.

There was no lichen, no blooms or tendrils within the main facility, but the entrance to the corridor linking to the Annexe was covered as if the lichen had grown to this point and decided it was done. I found a body at the threshold, untouched by lichen, wearing a hazmat suit and not moving.

Crouching down to pull it out from the corridor, a drum of sloshing liquid on its back got in the way. The drum was strapped on over the shoulders, so I rolled them off on each side and noted the black flame on an orange background painted on the side. The body was still heavy and the Perspex front to their head gear was blackened so I couldn't see if they were alive but I didn't dare spend time removing it so close to the lichen.

With a heave, the body moved backwards as I strained until we were clear of the corridor and in the main facility proper. As if it had been waiting for this moment, the lichen shrivelled up, retreating from us back down the corridor and into the Annexe. As it disappeared inside, the door to the Annexe at the far end of the corridor pulled shut and the lights came on all around.

Squinting under the glare, I saw scorch marks on the walls and ashes piled on the floor.

I could see that the drum of liquid was connected to a thin pipe ending on a solid steel nozzle. They'd been burning the lichen.

I turned back to the prone body beside me, crouching down by the head I pushed fingers on the material protecting its neck, hoping in vain that it was thin enough to detect a pulse.

'What kind of idiot applies raw energy directly to an unknown material?'

'Step away from the body,' came a clear instruction in a firm voice.

'I'm trying to help.' I didn't look up.

'Step away. Now.'

I stopped moving as I thought about what I was achieving here, my forefinger and index finger held uselessly against the polymer suit. The answer being obvious, I stood up and stepped away.

At which point I was tackled to the ground and held there until the body I'd dragged from the corridor was stretchered away. With my face pushed into carpet tile I couldn't see anything of the two people sitting on my back and apart from turning my head to breathe more easily that was the last I saw of the person I'd saved from the lichen.

Part 3 – Anger

Seven

The decontamination process took just as long the second time. The power of bureaucracy is that it reduces everyone it encounters down to interchangeable pieces that can be dealt with consistently without the inconvenience of considering their individuality.

And so I was sitting once again in the tent dressed in a new set of loose fitting cotton sweatshirt and slacks.

No one spoke and a woman with a beret and rifle stood by the exit who'd not been there the last time I was in the room. She didn't look in my direction but her very presence forcefully caged any thoughts of leaving. She was young enough to be my child, her face carelessly free of blemishes.

I thought about the body I'd pulled back from the threshold, about what they had been trying to do. Had the intruder attempted to spread beyond the Annexe? Was it so corny and devastating a possibility that they were truly invading, that I was living in an HG Wells novel come to life? I thought about the similarity of the lichen to the Red Weed and Wells' startling idea of terraforming aliens before there was even a word for the concept he was describing.

I shook my head; Red Weed and the lichen were different; the lichen had agency, it had pursued power, sought after Rhona once they'd made contact. Whatever else the lichen might be it wasn't an incidental or a consequence, it was the thing itself. *Das Ding an Sich* as Kant would have said.

What had happened to Rhona? Where was she?

Adeola was clear; there was no sign of the lichen or Rhona on their thermal imaging. Except I realised she was talking bullshit. They'd been burning the lichen which meant they knew it was there and if it was there then so was Rhona.

Why would they lie to me like that? I'd been left questioning my own understanding of what had happened to me. Adeola had arrived and, despite not even having been there when the lichen first appeared, succeeded in making me feel like she knew more than I did about what I'd been through. The thought that it was so easy to unseat my own experience turned my stomach. I decided it was because she spoke with such casual authority, like someone so used to being in charge that the rest of us accept the idea without even questioning it; assuming they know more even though they know nothing more than they've been told. It occurred to me that I was vulnerable, probably in shock, and the possibility that they'd deliberately taken advantage made me angry. Not that there was anything I could with that emotion; I was sitting in a room with a young woman whose blank focus suggested her entire vocabulary consisted of 'Yes' and 'Sir'.

Without a phone I had no way of gauging the passage of time but it felt slow. The image of Rhona by the door to the Annexe, the thing that had co-opted her body, the emptiness of her eyes; these were the things I couldn't get past, couldn't shake from my mind.

They came for me eventually; Adeola their representative. She was dressed in a suit this time, her military fatigues swapped for the nondescript uniform of civilians everywhere. Being dry and dressed, I had a better chance to take her in. She wore no rings, nothing in her ears either. With a beckoning hand she led me from the tent and into the facility. Akshai and I, together with the tech team who supported us worked on the ground and first floor – we had a direct route to the Annexe. I followed her up stairs to the fourth floor, a thin film of sweat pooling under my arms.

The room she left me in had no windows, lit by a ring of dull LEDs set into the roof. A single desk sat in the centre with one chair facing two on the other side. A bottle of water and four empty glasses collected dew at one edge.

The floor was scuffed, the carpet tiles scarred and depressed from furniture that had been there until mere moments before I arrived. It reminded me of a police interview room except there was no one-way mirror on the wall and no camera in a corner of the ceiling. They'd even taken off the name plate for whoever's office it had been before they'd taken it over.

They found me with my hands on my hips, staring at the table. Sitting down felt like an admission that they were in charge and I was their thing to do with as they pleased, so I stood for as long as they'd let me.

Adeola returned with another who was only marginally more interesting to look at. Her most interesting feature was a nose that had seen one too many scrums at school and ears that had been grabbed for purchase so much that they'd lost all shape. She was tall, tightly built but with the creeping softness that no amount of gym time can get rid of once a sedentary lifestyle sinks its roots in.

They sat opposite me and we skated on the edge of awkwardness while they poured water.

Neither of them had notepads or tablets. I assumed there was a camera of which I wasn't aware, otherwise they were just subtly bullying me with how they were able to soak up anything I might have to say without making notes.

They introduced themselves as Adeola and Joan.

They had me run over my name, my address and my occupation. We talked about how long I'd been working for the company, about how I'd found my way there. Adeola didn't mention that we'd spoken earlier in the same way one might not explain their familiarity to a pigeon they'd fed bread to previously.

Their sedate approach was meandering, appearing to get lost on minor points but, at the same time, they moved swiftly from one subject to another with a focus I recognised as similar to that I used when interviewing PhD candidates for their vivas. A friend of mine described it as checking the fence posts were both straight and deep enough into the earth.

'What were you doing here tonight?' Asked Adeola.

'I was working as normal. Akshai was in the lab. Before I left I checked she was okay but it was just another evening.' Adeola's expression was flat at my statement but in her thin straight mouth I could see she was asking me to stop suggesting anything about the night was normal.

'Would you say you were making progress with your research?' Asked Joan.

I frowned, uncertain what the point of the question was. The director's comment about how the night would go came back to me, so I held my frustration with questions about which I couldn't see a point and answered them.

'Yes. My research has three goals, although two are unlooked for benefits arising from the type of work we're doing.'

'What do you mean?' Asked Adeola.

'I'm working toward strong encryption methods using quantum kernels and, ultimately, keys that don't need the recipient to have access to the same technology that created the encryption in the first place.'

'Can you explain that for us?' Asked Joan.

'When did you last do maths?' I asked, hoping it wasn't the most common answer I got at any and all parties I went to with Rhona, 'oh I haven't done any since I was fourteen'.

'Assume we're educated amateurs,' said Adeola.

'Qubits, the quantum unit of information we're trying to use in quantum computing, can have greater than N bits of information but they can only translate N bits back to a classical information receiver. I realise that's kind of backwards, that you might want to think of it as we take N bits and have them held by a Qubit which, itself, can carry more than just that information. Think of it like putting water into a bucket one cup at a time. You can put more than one cup of water into a bucket but regardless of the amount of water you've put in, your cup can only take one cup of water back out of the bucket at a time. This was figured out by Holveo. The trick we're trying to achieve here is to pump our Qubits full of information and then ensure that we can get the bits we want, and just those bits, back out of it at the time and place we want them.'

'Why's that hard?' Asked Joan.

The question was dumb, the analogy I'd used about the cup and bucket made that obvious, but I decided she was actually interested so kept going. However, the longer I spoke the more I wondered why they were asking me about my work and the more my words grated in my own ears like the scraping together of broken seashells.

'Because we don't really know how information is carried, just that it is. We're trying to get the exact same cup of water out as the one we put in, all the same molecules which mix with all the others already in the bucket. There are schools of thought that information isn't even real although most people believe it is, in some sense, fundamental.'

'If lots of people think that, what makes you different?' Asked Adeola.

'What makes you worth all this?' Asked Joan if we were investment bankers expensing oysters and champagne.

'This is where our research is a confluence of beneficial outcomes. Our goal is the sea of strong encryption but the rivers we're taking to get there are quantum information theory and group theory.' I stopped as neither of them were nodding along any more. We needed to take a mental step back. 'Look, there's this paradox about information that most people think has kind of been solved now; it was the basis of one of the most famous bets in science of the last century.'

Still nothing.

'Right. You've heard of Stephen Hawking, yes?' They both nodded. 'Well he suggested that blackholes evaporate, send out all the energy inside them and eventually just disappear. The problem was that everything has information within it – the photon, the electromagnetic wave, the piece of dust – it's all information. Inside the blackhole it looked like everything was totally jumbled up worse than a box of Lego pieces. That moment when you fall into the blackhole is like a point where you take a block of cheese and grate it. After it's happened, how can you possibly say that this piece of cheese went there in the block? Totally impossible right?' I shifted in my chair, wanting to finish quickly but knowing I had to bring them with me. 'But we have this other idea that information can't be created or destroyed, so how does a blackhole do it and then re-emit all this energy out the other side?'

'I thought it was energy that couldn't be created or destroyed,' said Adeola.

'It is that,' said Joan firmly, as if I'd just lied to them and they'd caught me red handed.

But I was used to this kind of reaction. 'Ah, but that's the point, right? What if the reason energy can't be created or destroyed is because, it is, basically, the units by which information interacts with itself.'

'What do you mean?' asked Adeola.

'Let me put it another way. We run simulations of blackholes with a unique solution we believe will solve the paradox quantitatively and hence give us the key to strong encryption while also telling us a huge amount about how the universe works.' I quoted directly from our pitch book to investors. 'Not only do we make the first true strong quantum encryption which can be used by anyone even if they don't have the tech, we break an entirely new field of physics into the mainstream. Money and accolades.'

'You're saying that everything has information,' said Joan slowly. I had a sudden image of her being told by a restaurant that they'd not held her reservation.

'No.' I held my finger up, glad to be at the point of it all. 'I'm saying that information describes everything, at its most fundamental level. A theologian called Tillich had this idea he called the Ground of Being, the very thing from which everything else finds its existence proceeding. He called it God. I'm calling it information. Energy comes from information and how that information expresses itself, not the other way around. Energy doesn't have information, energy *is* information in a certain form.'

'This gets you around your paradox?' Asked Adeola. The meaning of what I'd said wasn't important to her, just the implications.

'It does, because it says the information falling into the blackhole isn't lost, it's just reconfigured like scrunching up a ball of paper that can then be straightened out again when it comes out. If we can show that, we get the gold star.'

'How did you know about the Rio Scale?' Asked Joan, her eyes cutting away and shutting the subject down completely.

'That's the third part of what we're doing. Look, the universe is vast and we're tiny. We can't travel faster than light, we can't make warp drives and the energy required to get people, alive, out of the solar system is beyond our practical resources, regardless of theory. It may stay that way forever. But what if that's true for everyone out there? What if they work out that information is fundamental too? Isn't there a chance we could find them deep in the information?'

'This is the third of your research legs?' Asked Adeola.

'This is nonsense,' said Joan with a hiss. 'Information is artificial. The numbers in your computer are on your hard disk in actual locations. They're not real by themselves.'

Adeola frowned at Joan, the mask of detachment slipping for a moment to reveal an irritation with her partner.

As the words left my mouth I regretted how flippantly I said them. 'The Annexe would say I'm right and you're wrong.'

Joan gave me a disgusted look that told me we'd arrived at what they wanted to really talk about.

'You're happy to confirm that you were attempting to contact non-human life.' She stated it as a fact while, by her side, Adeola lent forward and stared at me. I could have been a bowl of agar jelly under a microscope.

'What? No. We never expected any of this.' I put my hands on the table, struggling to control my anger. In a low voice I managed to say, 'my wife was here tonight.'

'We'll get to that,' said Adeola kindly. 'For now, please concentrate on the question you're being asked.'

'I've answered it.'

'But you were anticipating that as a potential outcome.' Joan said the words like she was asking if I'd realised that drinking while driving might lead to a fatal accident.

'Look, we joked about it. Was I seriously thinking about meeting aliens? Of course not.'

'Do you think Akshai thought you'd meet aliens? Was that why she was here alone tonight?' asked Adeola.

'I can't say what she was thinking. She was running a new set of servers we'd had installed that allowed us to run the largest set of simulations yet.'

'I'd think that since you were sleeping with her you'd have a good idea of what she was hoping to achieve,' said Joan.

'Did your wife, Rhona, know about the affair?' Asked Adeola.

My throat closed and it was all I could to swallow without giving in to the retch that sat at the back of my tongue like a gremlin wanting to take control.

The corners of Joan's mouth twitched up in the slightest of smiles.

'Tell us about why you came back,' she asked. They listened in silence as I told the story.

'Shouldn't removing a large subroutine lead to problems in running the simulation?' asked Adeola.

'Not necessarily. Good code is written in blocks which can be slid about and slotted together as you need them, It's like building a house; most of it's bricks with very few bits that need specific shapes that have to go in just one place. The routine we removed to test what was going wrong had been added later. We'd built the software to work without it originally.'

'Isn't it true you knew it would sabotage the simulations?' said Joan.

I didn't answer. How could I respond to the question with any sort of meaningful answer?

'Did you know?' Asked Adeola.

'I didn't make this happen,' I spluttered, trying to get to the heart of the accusation. 'I've worked for the company for years. Why would I jeopardise my career over something so unlikely there's no way I could have predicted it?' I slapped the table in frustration. 'This is stupid. I haven't done anything.'

'Then why did you return later with Rhona? If you didn't know?' asked Joan. 'Is she actually as sick as you claim? Or is that another way you sought to deceive the company?'

'She's dying,' I said, the first time I'd ever said the words out loud. Their finality filled the room with darkness. 'She's still in there. Why aren't you asking me about that? Why aren't you trying to get her back?'

'So tell us,' said Adeola. 'Tell us what happened when you came back with her.'

I listened to her words but couldn't shake the sharpness of their eyes as they cut each word I spoke a dozen different ways. My core was piling up with frustration and fear, a pillar of white noise in my soul that was slowly building in volume so that thinking clearly demanded more and more of my attention, but what could I do except answer their questions until they ran out?

Eight

The words sounded ridiculous and utterly insufficient at the same time. I was trying to explain the colour red to the blind. They listened without interrupting until I reached the point of fleeing the lab and leaving Rhona behind.

'You admit damaging the data centre,' said Joan after I'd finished. 'You admit you would have done worse if you could have figured out a way.'

'We were trying to contain the event.'

'What event?' Asked Adeola, her face expressionless.

I couldn't believe they were asking. 'Everything I've just told you,' I said, my voice rising. 'Why are we having this stupid discussion while the Annexe is full of non-human life? Or would you rather I'd just walked away and let it continue?'

'That is what you did,' said Joan. 'We found you outside the Annexe. You'd even left your wife inside, alone. Did you plan for her to die when you did this?'

'Piss off,' I spat at her. I expected to cry but instead I wanted to rip her carefully bland face from her skull. 'I love her.'

'From the outside it looks like you were getting ready to leave her,' said Adeola. 'Joan doesn't mean to be antagonistic but you're sleeping with Ms. Slim and have been for more than two months. Are you saying you love them both?'

Did I love Akshai? If I did it wasn't like Rhona; we'd been together nearly twenty years, since we'd met at university. We'd been through life, were growing old together. I'd stayed with her when she got ill, when it became obvious she was going to die before she turned forty and that her death would be slow, painful and humiliating. When her own family grew tired of visiting their dying daughter I was still there. How could they question my loyalty?

Akshai had been there when I needed to talk, when I'd needed to cry but couldn't bear to let Rhona know how selfish I was being. I'd not meant for anything to happen; she was ten years younger than me and wasn't my type, but one night after Rhona had responded horrifically to the latest round of therapy we'd got drunk together and somehow ended up in bed.

The sense of guilt and release had been a plug coming lose within me and a mixture of black gunk rushing out on a stream of pleasure.

'Ms Shannon?' Asked Joan, her head cocked so her eyes could meet mine. 'Do you love Ms. Slim?'

'We've been seeing each other. I've been with Rhona for eighteen years.'

'Were you faithful all that time?' Asked Adeola.

'Would you be asking a man these questions?' I countered.

Joan shrugged. 'What we'd be doing if you were someone else isn't relevant. You're here. Now. So please answer the questions.'

'Yes,' I said, hating myself for continuing to cooperate. I was a ship without a rudder.

'Why didn't you call us earlier?' Asked Adeola.

'Nothing seemed like it was out of control.' Which was hardly true but I didn't have an answer that satisfied me let alone them.

'You'd fled the campus, gone to see your wife and, in breach of your contract, told her about what happened,' said Joan.

'Then you brought her back here,' said Adeola.

'What were you thinking?' Joan asked.

I shook my head. 'She wanted to see it.' I waved my hands vaguely in the direction of the Annexe. 'What we'd done. She wanted to see the keyboard melted into lichen and glass. I didn't want to bring her but she's got so little time left what was I going to say?'

'You could have said no,' Adeola replied.

'What would you know about it?' I shot back. 'She's been fighting this for two years. And she's lost. Every step someone was there to tell us there was more to do, further to go, other medicines and techniques to try. Until there wasn't. One day we found ourselves alone in the consulting room with no news except the worst kind, our hopes exhausted and lying dead among the latest report of failure from yet another horrible cocktail of drugs whose side effects were as harsh as anything her illness put her through.'

'She would have died earlier without them,' said Joan, the kindness in her voice catching me off guard.

'Would she?' I rubbed at the skin on the back of my hand with my thumb. 'It doesn't matter now does it? We're here and the rest is useless speculation.'

'So why did you bring her?' Continued Adeola.

'I don't know. Because I'm not in a place to tell her no? Could you have looked her in the eyes and denied the stupid desire to have a sense of wonder rekindled on the edge of death? I hate that you think I might have done this on purpose, but I didn't.' I sighed as I realised why I'd brought her. 'I did this for love.'

The room was silent for a few moments.

'Even love has consequences,' said Joan.

At some unseen signal they stood up together. 'This part of the interview is complete.'

'What now?' I asked, finding enough resentment to remain seated while they were standing.

'You'll be dropped at home. You're no longer needed here. Once we're done you'll be brought back in for the next stage of the debrief.' Adeola turned toward the door, effectively dismissing me.

'You can't send me home. I know what happened to cause this.' I wasn't going to be sent to the naughty step while the company interfered with my work without any sense they were doing it to get Rhona back.

The car that dropped me off had blacked out windows and, if anyone in the street was watching, struck me as utterly out of place in my part of the city. The driver waited for me to open the front door before they drove away.

Their last words blocked up my ears all the way home. 'We don't need you,' finished Adeola, leaving the room.

'You're part of the problem,' said Joan.

The sky was growing light, the palest blues and pinks scaring away the stars before the sun came to bring its fullest glory. The air was cool outside and stale when I stepped into the hallway. I could smell cold soup, dust, loneliness.

Sleep poked and prodded at my consciousness, but I couldn't stop thinking about what had happened.

I was in the kitchen, a cup on the side as I made coffee. The pan in which I'd warmed last night's dinner was thick with what I'd not eaten.

Having nothing better to do, I washed it up, finding the bowl on the table I washed that too. Halfway through I saw myself as if from above, watched the dirty bowl in my hands, saw the bubbles on the water and wanted to know why I was wasting my time with such meaninglessness.

I gripped the cup with both hands and stared at the woman in the window. She looked wrung out, her dark olive skin the pallor of damp dishcloth, her curly hair hanging limp around her face. Yet it wasn't the physical signs of exhaustion that really stood out; I couldn't see anything in my own face, nothing I recognised as me.

'Don't talk to anyone until we release you,' the driver had said as I got out. 'That means do not attempt to contact Ms Slim.'

'What if the phone rings? I've got thirteen messages from the hospice.' I'd asked snarkily checking my newly returned handset for obvious signs they'd tampered with it.

'Ignore it. Better still, switch it off until advised otherwise. Don't talk to anyone, don't even answer the door.'

Which left me without a response, witty or otherwise.

I resisted the urge to throw the cup across the room or smash it in the sink. Instead I filled a glass of water and drank it straight down. Then I smashed the glass in the sink, a deliberate, forceful throw accompanied by a roar of everything inside me.

It didn't clear my head. Rather, the cotton wool that was filling my mind took on a sharper tone, a blizzard that froze what it touched.

My hand was hot and cold at the same time, the skin crawling as if a fly were dancing across it. Splashes of scarlet were collecting among the broken glass. Examining the gash in my palm I pulled a piece of kitchen towel from the work surface and held it against the wound. Now that I'd seen it, the cut stung and I held my fingers still so as not to cause myself more pain.

I switched on the radio with an elbow on my way to the kitchen table but stopped as soon as I heard the music; it was a station Akshai had chosen, full of energetic pop and millennials talking as if everything couldn't get better.

Restored to silence I sat at the table, hand elevated and listened to my own breathing.

'Don't leave me,' I said to the air. After all the waiting, after all the despair, Rhona had vanished in front of my eyes while I stood powerless to help. There was sound inside me, curled up in my gut, incoherent and raging.

I opened my mouth to scream but couldn't start. The urge hovered on my shoulder, whispering to me that it was the right thing to do but I couldn't see how it would change anything. The company would still be done with me, Rhona would still be gone, and I'd still be sat in my kitchen, discarded with no right of reply.

The paper towel stuck to my hand; time to dress the wound properly. Since the illness our bathroom had become a pharmacy where people occasionally brushed their teeth. Working one handed was awkward but eventually I had my hand wrapped up. The presence of the mirror over the bathroom sink irritated me; I didn't want reminding that I was there, alone, in the house. Each glimpse I caught told me I wasn't at the facility trying to get Rhona back, that Akshai and I had been split up by people who didn't understand what they were doing.

I was disturbed by the sound of movement from downstairs.

Calling out there was no answer but the continued sounds of someone opening cupboards and the clink of mugs.

There wasn't so much as a makeshift weapon in the house, the best I could do was switch on the lights as I descended the stairs. The doorway to the kitchen was open and I watched in disbelief.

'You didn't drink your coffee,' said Rhona, coming to the edge of the room to greet me. 'Do you want another or shall I warm that one up for you? It's barely cold.' Seeing that I couldn't answer her she walked back into the kitchen. 'C'mon now, come and sit down with me.'

Did it matter that she wasn't there? It wasn't her, it didn't feel like her, but the temptation to give in to whatever ghosts my brain was conjuring was so, so strong. I followed her into the kitchen. Would it dispel the illusion if I put my hand through it? Except we bumped up against one another when I judged the distance wrong.

Rhona laughed and wrapped her arms around me. We stayed like that for a long time, my eyes open, conscious of the feel of her green cardigan against my cheek but unwilling to break the spell.

Eventually she led me to the table, sat me down. 'You hurt your hand,' she said without a drop of sympathy.

I watched her face, the way she moved. It was almost her but not quite. Whatever she was, this Rhona was caught in the uncanny valley where she was just real enough to make me feel uncomfortable. Her eyes were a degree off the right green. Her accent a whisker too Dubliner, not enough Cork. Her shoulders were straight back rather than having the slight hunch she carried because she didn't want to appear as tall as she really was.

'What are we doing?' I asked.

'We, I, us,' she started and then I knew what was sharing my house with me. 'Are present among you because of this one. Your one. It bleeds through into us, me, all and so our conversation has, must, ought to occur with you. You are separated but your information is entangled.'

'She would have said that two had become one,' I replied. 'Rhona is an artist.' As if that would explain why she'd think it but I wouldn't.

'Her equation of state includes elements of you. We have informed those others like you that we will talk to you alone.'

I laughed with a hollow sense of exultation. How would Adeola and Joan feel about that kind of demand?

'I want her back,' I said.

'Her form is impaired, her information about to fracture into new forms. Time does not run backwards.'

'Can you give her back to me?' I asked, cursing myself for the stupidity of hoping they could cure cancer, that they would cure it for me. The possibility, the fear it was mistaken, balled up in me, my own black cancer that touched every part with its corruption.

Rhona did not answer. Instead she took my reheated coffee from the microwave and put it on the table. 'Time cannot run backwards.'

'But it can,' I said, my voice breaking. 'We showed that a long time ago.'

'Take me to there, show me the people proving it,' she said. I thought she was mocking me but in her emotionless face there was nothing malicious.

Before I could stop I was holding her, my arms grasping her torso as deep wretched howls of pain filled my kitchen.

I didn't remember the tears stopping but eventually there was nothing left inside that could come out. I was a shopping bag used one too many times.

My mobile rang, vibrating from within my bag. It had to be the company and I had to answer it. Time didn't run backwards.

'I should answer that.'

Rhona's arms let me go. The phone stopped buzzing before I got to it, battling my way through everything else that was in there. It was the Director's personal number.

I looked up to say I needed to ring her back but Rhona, or whatever had brought her shape to me, was gone. At the corners of my vision, as intangible as distantly glimpsed reflections might have been a crowd of faces staring back at me. A moment later they too were gone.

'Sarah,' said the Director. 'I hope you were sleeping.' She stopped. 'I mean, I didn't want to wake you but I hope you found some time to rest.' I smiled on my end of the line; it was good to have someone else feeling awkward. 'How, how are you doing?'

'I'm okay,' I said and realised it was approximately true.

Silence followed, as if she'd forgotten that she was the one who'd rung me.

'How can I help?' I asked as evenly as I could manage.

'We need you back here. I'm going to send someone as soon as we're off the line. If you're willing.'

'Why wouldn't I be willing?' Although I could name a dozen reasons not to go back, the chance to see Rhona again overrode every other concern.

'It's been a long night,' said the Director as if that explained everything.

'Can I have time to shower and change?' I asked.

'Of course,' she said too quickly. 'We'll have breakfast here for you too. You like bircher don't you?'

'Honestly? I want eggs, sausage and bacon.'

She agreed with me that my choice was excellent.

'What happened?' I asked as she was wrapping up.

She stumbled over her sentence before spinning to a stop. 'You're needed here. We think you have a unique role in dealing with this. We'll brief you properly in person. You understand.'

'I understand,' I replied, when of course I had no idea what she meant. The harsh truth as far as I could see was that she didn't need me, the company didn't need me. There was a globally recognised response protocol for meeting non-human intelligence and it could operate via anyone. Which was the whole point.

'What about Rhona?' I asked at last.

'We hope to retrieve her. There are signs we can do just that and we remain confident that there are plenty of options for us to try. There is always hope,' said the Director.

I hung up with something else ringing in my mind; that hope deferred makes the heart grow sick, that hope extinguished brings the darkest of nights for the soul.

Nine

The rush hour roads were so clogged with traffic it took nearly an hour to make the five-mile journey to site. The city was busy around us as we crawled along, a melange of harsh colour and grating noise stopping and starting according to its own rhythm, carrying on regardless of the events at the facility.

As I stepped from the car, the warm air and clean sunshine gave the campus an elysian feel. Glaziers were working on the main facility and had already replaced the ground floor's windows. The car park was full but with black cars instead of the normal mishmash of makes and colours.

How much privacy did the company have? I wondered, impressed at how quickly they'd found half a dozen people to work on the building in the few hours I'd been away, at the lack of police cars and media.

Did the owners of the office park know what the company was doing or what was happening within the Annexe? Was there anything they could have done if they did know what was happening on their property?

As I was walked into the building I could hear accents from around the world; American, German, Dutch and Nordic among others. The hazmats were gone, the offices repopulated by people in suits; talking, moving furniture or sitting and working at computers.

Adeola met me by the ground floor reception, dismissing the driver who'd stayed at my side from the moment I'd left the car. This time we settled in a conference room with a view overlooking the fields backing onto the office park and whose windows had been replaced.

True to the Director's promise, there were bacon butties, sausages and eggs on a plate under a plastic dome waiting for me. The smell that greeted me when I lifted the lid was almost perfect.

Adeola asked if I wanted a coffee and left to go find it. She didn't return until I'd finished breakfast; she had two ceramic cups, one of which she placed in front of me before sitting down on the other side of the long oval table. It had 'I heart spreadsheets' on the side.

'Thank you for coming back in,' she said. There was no sign of contrition in her expression but it was gratifying to see her looking as tired as I felt.

'Why am I back?' I asked.

'We have some more questions for you.'

'Really?' I asked, bemused that she would continue with her previous evasiveness. 'I assumed it was because you needed me.'

'Would you be prepared to answer some more questions?' She persisted.

'You're not in a call centre,' I said. 'You don't need to follow some useless script.'

She didn't say anything, so I tartly asked her, 'So you don't need my help?'

For the first time she shifted uncomfortably in her chair. 'We think you may be able to help us,' she admitted. 'But to know that for sure there's a lot we need to figure out.'

'No Joan today?'

She shook her head briskly, unruffled by my question. 'She has other tasks better suited to her skills.' Which was as much explanation as I'd resigned myself to receiving. They might need me but they weren't about to bring me into their club.

I pushed the empty plate to the side and lent on the table, hands clasped together. 'Ask away.'

'How is it possible that they were waiting within your simulations?'

'A good question. They weren't and haven't ever been in our simulations. Think of information like actual physical space. People occupy information space. This body I'm in is information composed a certain way, change it and I'm no longer me, I might not even be this body, but a table, or a fridge. Expressed the right way I'm a dog, an explosion or a vacuum. Our simulations were directly exploring information space. If it was me and I wanted to find other intelligent life I'd not look at the sky, I'd look at information space.'

'For example?' She asked.

'Apart from the Annexe?' I stared at her until she looked away but she didn't move on so I thought about her question. 'Irrational numbers. What if, somewhere deep in root two or pi we find a repeating pattern? We'd know someone put it there.' I shrugged. 'The problem though is you'd be forced to conclude the universe was nothing more than a simulation.'

She frowned. 'Why?'

'We think that physics is pretty much the same everywhere, right? We can't be completely sure but if we didn't make that assumption there'd be no science. If someone changes pi or the value of two plus two, it changes everywhere. If someone put a pattern in a supposedly random number like pi…' I paused, wincing at how imprecise Adeola was forcing me to be. 'Then it would change everywhere. If that's the case then you'd need to be outside to make that kind of change without risk. So we'd assume that there was an outside and that someone there had made the inside.'

'So you'd prove God?'

'No. What?' The idea hadn't ever occurred to me. 'No, we'd just prove that you and I aren't any more real than a computer game character on someone else's computer.'

'Seems to me you've proved God,' said Adeola again.

'Look, the point is if you're here with the rest of us you change something that can be changed, that doesn't need you to have access to the whole estate. Or run the risk you disappear in a puff of improbability the moment you make the alteration. If you've realised that information is fundamental you might leave markers out there in information space, cowbells that trip when someone else comes poking around doing manipulations you think makes them suitably advanced to be worth having a chat with.'

'And your simulations of blackholes meet that criteria?'

'Maybe.' I said slowly. 'It might be half a dozen other things we did with the network. I can't say.'

'Then what?'

'I don't know.' I rolled my eyes, tripping on anger that wasn't as purged as I'd thought. 'They'd not be aliens if we could say. They'd be neighbours, conceptually at least even if not physically.'

'Can't they be neighbours?' Asked Adeola, trying to sound reasonable instead of completely out of her depth.

'Really? Whoever they are, they aren't physically local. They're smart enough to have put early warning systems for when racoons like us come poking around their bins. Who says they have to access information the way we do? We provoked this by accessing information space using a surrogate; a computer does the work for us. Do you really think that other species would have the same type of brain we do, that they'd think like us?'

'Why not? Your accounts of what happened include them streaming numbers and then equations across the monitors.'

'Numbers makes sense. Everything's going to count, it's how I know you're not me and I'm not you, because I can tell the difference between me and the rest of the world. Then the equations flow from there. They'll have understood the calculations we were performing, could probably have seen how we were expressing that information and then repurposed that to try to talk to us. Maths is their Rosetta stone.'

'They've got their own babel fish?' she asked.

'Very good,' I said. 'Yes, they could probably talk about abstract concepts with any species who has a working philosophy of maths.'

'Not just counting then, but a knowledge of why we count in the first place. They might struggle with emotions, perhaps?'

I thought about my conversations with the alternate Rhona, the way they'd been unable to pin down the idea of an individual. 'Possibly. They won't have any idea of our genders, our society or even that we're driven by a soup of neurones contained in a skull.'

'Can they be hurt?' she asked then, the words clear but unhappy ones. The question was so cliché I didn't know what to say. Seeing my reticence, Adeola continued. 'We have to consider the possibility that they mean us harm.'

'Why?' I asked, seeing Rhona standing in our kitchen, feeling her arms around my body like the warmth of hope on a faithless day.

'It's pretty easy to consider reasons why you'd overwhelm a technologically inferior community upon discovering them; they'd be poorly equipped to fight back, psychologically disadvantaged and, most of all, unaware of what real wealth they might have that you could reach out and take for yourselves. It would be colonialism on a galactic scale.'

'No,' I said, realising it was hard to argue against.

'There's no reason to assume that because you're technologically advanced you're benign; our history shows that we stay the same regardless of what weapons we've got in our hands. Why should they be any different?'

'What happened last night?' I asked.

'I can't talk about it.'

I considered getting up and leaving. A simple fuck you to people who still didn't get that all I wanted was Rhona and their obfuscation, their need to protect themselves, showed they'd happily betray me with every word uttered. Instead I waited, arms folded across my chest and silent.

It took Adeola five minutes to decide she could tell me. 'We wanted to seal the doors to the Annexe shut. As soon as the welding torch touched the entrance their lichen spread into the corridor. We turned the heat onto them but they responded by expanding exponentially.'

'Was that the body I dragged from the hallway?'

She nodded. 'No one died but fire isn't going to work. That much we know.'

'Of course it wouldn't work; you were giving them energy, raw information they could simply turn into something that worked for them here in our world.'

'Which is what we concluded too. A truck of liquid nitrogen is on its way here. Our first step will be to force them back into the Annexe and then we'll seal it from outside and create a vacuum within.'

'It's a plan with the merit of being a plan,' I said, sighing.

'You don't think it will work?' She sounded surprised.

'I have a rule for my grads and staff – don't make statements or ask questions that don't move the discussion on. They hate it at first.' I snorted. 'They probably hate it all the time but it forces them to think their ideas through before they come tumbling out of their mouths as the first thing that occurs to them.'

'We have the very best working on this,' replied Adeola curtly.

'I'm sure. Top people. What about the SETI protocol?'

'They took your wife. We're past benevolent visitors at this point.' She tapped her fingers on the table.

'You don't know that,' I said.

The tapping stopped. 'Why would you think that? Rhona's your wife.'

'Why wouldn't I stop hoping?'

'What happened? In there? What did they promise you?'

'Nothing happened. They took Rhona, she was compost into which they could plant their roots. But I want her back and attacking them means attacking her.' I stopped talking, thought about how to correct what I meant. 'It means attacking the Annexe. Turning the building into a vacuum will kill her.'

Adeola stood up. 'Let me be clear; we don't trust you. It's not a moral judgement, but you're compromised. We're dealing with a probable first contact situation and your questions are about whether your wife is safe. I get that, I do. But it makes my point for me.' She stopped then, perhaps waiting to see just how offended I was. 'Your Director's the only one who's stood up for you. We don't know what you did or said to the visitors but they've demanded to talk with you and only you.'

I had an image of Rhona standing on the threshold asking for me.

'How did they communicate with you? How do you know it has to be me?'

'Now you want to know,' said Adeola. 'When it's all about you.' She sat back down with a sigh, leaving her chair facing away, as if she meant to leave again as soon as she was done. 'What does it matter? We've been stuttering along using half a dozen different methods. They managed to convince the team that you're the one they need.'

'What about Akshai?' I wanted to know she was okay.

'We don't need her,' said Adeola.

82

'I need her.'

'I don't think you do. I think she's a port in a storm. When Rhona dies you won't want her around reminding you of how you betrayed her, of how, when you could have been at her side you were in Akshai's bed instead.'

I grabbed the plate on which they'd served my breakfast and threw it hard, past Adeola's head and against the wall. It cracked into pieces, shards flaying back across the room.

'You know nothing,' I shouted at her.

'You assume you're the only one who's ever lost someone they loved.' She was still, meeting my eyes with a fire of her own. 'I know how grief works,' she said calmly. 'Akshai is not coming back in.'

'Then I won't help.'

'Okay,' said Adeola. 'Are we done?' She couldn't mean it, but then who was I to say what the company would do if I pushed hard enough. She waited for me. 'Well Sarah? Are we done?'

I picked up the cup to throw that too.

'Going to smash everything are you?' said Adeola dismissively.

I held it in my hand, felt its smooth glaze against my fingers. 'We're not done. You won't fire her if you want my help.'

'Done,' said Adeola quickly and I realised they'd have given in if only I'd pushed them harder. 'In return you won't say anything to them about what we're planning. You have one main goal and that's to buy us enough time to put our own plan in place.'

'How long before the nitrogen arrives?'

'An hour.'

'How do you know they're not listening to us now?'

'They're not,' said Adeola.

'You have no idea,' I countered. If they could bring Rhona to my house they could be in the room. 'We've already told them we're vicious and unpredictable; if it were me I'd watch us, I'd listen in and see what they were planning. Whether they could be trusted.'

'Why should we be the saints?' Asked Adeola. 'Why should we wait for them to make the first move? We're outgunned here, they can travel across the universe using information. How are we supposed to beat them if we wait?'

'Don't you think they'd have attacked us already if they were planning to?'

'Now you're not thinking it through,' said Adeola. 'Why should they do it like that? What if they must regroup once they arrive? What if they want to see just what we're capable of or whether we have anything they need?'

'You're just making stories up to suit your argument,' I said.

'So are you, Sarah.' And she was right.

'Then let me find out what they want.'

'Sure. Just make sure you take at least an hour.'

'I can't let you do this.'

She laughed, a sore ratchet of surprise. 'You don't get to say. In the event of a hostile incursion the protocol is clear. I'm sorry, Sarah, but it's already decided.'

'What happens after?' I asked.

'The future's a foreign country. There's literally no one who knows how this is going to play out once news of it gets out.' She cut through the air with her hand. 'That's irrelevant. Our job is to focus on what's in front of us.' There was a knock at the door. Adeola didn't look but I waited for it to open.

The Director stepped into the room.

'Good morning, Sarah. Adeola, could you give us the room please?'

Adeola left without looking at me. When she was gone the Director took her place opposite me at the table.

'I'm so sorry it's come to this,' she said. 'We have tried everything we could to see if there was a non-violent route forward but they are completely unresponsive.'

'They want to talk to me?' I asked. She nodded, her deep clear eyes holding me as she did so. 'Why not wait until I've spoken to them?'

'We can't countenance a relationship built upon you. It's nothing personal but what if you died? What if you couldn't be here and they decided to go to war over it. They're too dangerous, too unpredictable.'

'It's got nothing to do with me; what you're really saying is that you can't control them.'

'We can't.'

'You realise how ridiculous that sounds?'

'If God walked out of that room and wouldn't do as we asked we'd respond the same way,' she said. 'It's what we are.' She walked over to the windows, her eyes fixed on the city beyond. 'You think all that gets the way it does by accident? Do you think none of it would change if we weren't thinking about how to control what comes through from the other side? There can't be two powers in this world, just us. Or them. Which side would you choose?'

'What about Rhona? Does your promise to me still stand?'

She held out her hand, beckoning for me to take hold of it. 'We've done everything we could. I promised you that much.'

'I'm not finished trying.'

'I know.'

'Is there nothing they can say to stop you from attacking them?'

'We're not trying to harm them, just trying to send them back wherever they came from.'

'It doesn't work like that,' I tried.

'It doesn't matter anymore. They're here and we don't want them here. However they came, they've got to go.'

'I don't think they're really here,' I said. The Director didn't respond except to look at her watch.

'The truck will be here in fifty minutes. After that there'll be some set-up to do but we'll come for you before that's finished. If you want to speak to them your time's running out.'

'I'm ready,' I said and we started toward the Annexe.

Part 4 – Bargaining

Ten

There was no walking into the Annexe. Adeola was waiting outside the interview room and rather than walk me over to the lab she took me upstairs to where dozens of people were working in the open plan office.

A moon mission's worth of equipment was set up, crowding the walkways between the desks that were part of the facility's own lay out so we had to squeeze sideways to get across the room.

One corner of the floor had been cleared of desks, in their place were new machines brought in by the company. Thick cables ran down and along the floor before exiting the building through one of the broken windows.

A woman in a light grey shirt and dark skirt with blond hair looped back in a ponytail greeted us.

'You're Shannon?' she asked me, her eyes starting at mine but travelling the length of my body the way a tailor would check out a new customer. When I nodded she held out a clean hazmat.

'It won't help,' I said.

'It might,' she said. 'What you don't know is the clothes you wore when it first started were contaminated. Nothing we've tried has cleared it.' I swallowed, remembering that touch on my shoulder. She saw something in my face and her voice spiked up in surprise. 'You knew?'

I hadn't been certain; there had been no time to think about it.

She took my silence as permission to do what she wanted. 'You'll wear that because we can dispose of it afterwards. It's got a radio mike so we can talk to you as well as see and hear what you're experiencing.'

A fist closed around my stomach at the realisation they'd see Rhona.

'We don't know if the air's safe to breathe, so you'll be connected to us via an umbilical which will also provide you oxygen and monitor your heart rate.' She smiled but it was a ghost laid carelessly upon the profound seriousness that shaped the rest of her face. 'We'll be watching out for you. Any sign of trouble and we'll pull you out. Literally if necessary.'

I took the suit, looking around for somewhere to change.

She chuckled; it was the kindest sound I'd heard in days. 'Just put it on over what you're wearing. It'll be cosy but you do not want to be naked and sweating inside this thing.'

I wanted to ask someone why all this was happening to me. It seemed there was nothing I could do to control my fate.

But there wasn't anyone to ask. The people in the room were doing, but like me they had no choice in their roles; it was too late to decide anything, we were a collection of people living out consequences of decisions made elsewhere at other times.

And then Akshai was there. She stood before me like a child not sure of how her parents were going to receive her. Inside it was all I could do not to break at seeing her. Instead we embraced, shaking our heads at the madness we'd experienced since last we'd seen each other. She took me down to the corridor connecting the Annexe.

'They let me come to help you. I thought they were going to fire me but instead...' She trailed off, her jaw setting as she refocussed. 'We'll connect you up here,' she said, her hand on my arm. 'Among people who know what's going on we're not going to be remembered.' It struck me the words were supposed to be encouraging.

'I'm going to talk to them,' I said, determined to make some kind of difference, to have a say in what might happen next.

'There's nothing you can do except this,' she said. 'They've told me what they're going to do.' Her tone was flat, refusing to confirm how she felt about their intentions.

'You'll be listening. I know they can change the company's minds.' Even if I couldn't.

'Aren't you scared?' She asked suddenly.

The question shocked me; I was fixed on getting to Rhona, what did it matter?

The answer was easy, my gut was curled up into a stone and surrounded by a lightness which made me wonder if I'd throw up inside the suit once I'd put the helmet on, but Rhona was waiting for me to save her. 'You've given up on getting Rhona back, but I haven't. It's all that matters.'

She nodded. 'I practice mindfulness, on how to live in the moment, to take control of it. There's this exercise where we're encouraged to think of feelings we need to control as being managed by a big switch in ours heads. I've always struggled to see how that works but maybe you have to have a reason, something else to choose.' She hesitated, looking away from me. 'They say Rhona came to them, demanded to see you. That it wasn't her but nothing else they've tried has worked.'

My chest tightened, stopping me from speaking.

'I can't replace her,' she said but the words weren't meant for me. 'I'm sorry, Akshai.'

She shook her head. 'I was stupid to think I could help you.'

It was my turn to hold her but the best I could manage was to play a gloved hand on her cheek. 'I don't know where I would be without you.'

Our eyes met and I could see the empty plains within her soul. 'It's not enough.' Akshai's face shifted around as if she might say more but after a moment she gave me the last piece of the suit and crouched down to connect the umbilical.

The helmet was airtight and as the seals connected I lost all sense of the world beyond my body. My only portal out was the perspex panel in the front of the mask but it cut off all apart from the view straight ahead. It smelled like rubber gloves and talcum powder and I could feel the moisture in my breath collecting on the inside surface.

'Hello? Can you hear me?' It was Akshai on the internal intercom, her voice distorted by the suit.

There were fewer checks than I anticipated and after Akshai patted me down she pointed me in the direction of the Annexe corridor with two thumbs up.

The doors to the hallway were closed. On my side were cameras in tripods and bright halogen lights pointing at the Annexe. A couple of women were monitoring the other side via small displays. I could see temperature gauges, humidity readings even footage in a fuzzy greyscale.

One of them opened the doors and through I went.

To my surprise the lichen was gone. The brickwork was bare and the lights nothing more than the drab under-illumination I experienced each and every other day.

I couldn't see the ground at my feet through the visor and felt I'd fall over if my stride was too large. Going slowly gave me ample time to think on what I might find in the Annexe; I couldn't imagine it having changed except that Rhona would be standing there waiting for me. My soul itched at the thought.

'I'm at the door.' They'd not opened for me and I stood there like an idiot while they didn't respond.

'Sorry,' said one of the women monitoring the hallway. 'This is your last chance to turn back.'

The idea that I might choose not to go in surprised me. I turned to see down the corridor but they'd closed the outer doors behind me, the soft brushes closing over the top of the umbilical.

'Sarah, how are you doing?' It was the Director.

'I'm about to go speak with aliens.'

'We have a team here listening to your feed.' Of course they did. 'But in addition, I've got someone here who's going to support you.'

'Sarah?' It was Akshai. Her familiar focus on the S at the beginning of my name was so welcome I had to swallow to stop tears of relief springing from my eyes.

'Hi,' was all I managed.

'Are you ready?'

'If people keep asking me, the answer will eventually be no,' I said, knowing she'd understand.

The doors opened up, revealing a room lit by a soft warm glow that suffused the air like a spring morning filled with dandelion pollen. There was no sign of Rhona.

'When did this happen?' I asked them.

'We haven't seen inside there at all. Apart from you, no one else has been inside.' It was Adeola who spoke.

'Is that not what you saw yesterday?' Asked the Director.

'Akshai?' I asked, hoping she'd step up and explain, again, what we'd both seen.

She started to talk and I asked them to mute the channel so I could concentrate. There was no sign of the lichen, no pulsing limbs, no waving fronds searching for purchase.

The data room was gone. In place of server racks were plants; soft grasses that moved under their own volition, longer stemmed flowers whose buds had grown and already bloomed in the hours since I'd last been here.

The colours were those of a wildflower meadow: blues, lilacs, whites and butterscotch. They had small petals, nothing bigger than the largest coin I could think of. Except they weren't quite the right shapes; oblong petals, hexagonal pistels from which multi-jointed stamen reached and flexed for a sun they couldn't see.

The colonisation of the hall ended at the doors, a small semicircle of the original floor visible.

'Are you getting all this?' I asked.

'Yes,' said someone whose voice I didn't recognise.

'I'm going in.' My first step was slow, careful, even more so than demanded by the hazmat. I could hear my breathing in my ears, the other side of the membrane was silent and beyond me. An urge to take off the helmet sat at the back of my mind whispering its temptation.

I crouched down at the edge of the grasses; they leaned towards my fingers as I stretched out, as if they desired my touch. I wasn't there to pet a mat of grass and, levering my fingers under their roots, lifted. Beneath them was the lichen, dull now, emitting no light, as if its job was done.

I lay the grass back down carefully and got to my feet.

'The lichen's here, underneath it all.'

'They're terraforming the Annexe,' said Akshai.

I moved into the room; for all the plant life, the layout remained the same, with piles of greenery bulking up where the server racks had once formed the internal walls.

The desk was still there, thick tubes of lichen wrapped around one another like an oil tanker's anchor chain, dropping down from the screen bank which was also as we'd left it. The grasses started at the foot of the desk.

It took me a moment to realise that Rhona wasn't there. The chair in which they'd caught her was gone as well, replaced by waving grasses with bulbous seed heads whose thin luminous stems were barely keeping them upright.

'These people love their light,' I said.

'There are three theories as to why,' said Adeola. 'The best one is that they use it to communicate.'

'We, us, I need to talk to you in person,' said a voice through my intercom.

'Did you hear that?' I asked.

'What?' Asked Adeola.

'The voice, the one asking to talk to me in person?'

'Take your helmet off so we, those collected, community might speak directly,' it said.

'We can't hear anything,' said Adeola. 'Are you sure?'

'Is there interference?' Asked someone else.

'No. It's clear. It's them,' I said.

'There's nothing,' said someone else. There were too many people for me to hear anyone clearly.

'Can you all just get off the line,' I shouted. 'Adeola, Akshai, stay on.'

'Stay calm,' said Adeola. 'What are they saying?'

'If you can speak to me like this why do you want me to take my helmet off?' I asked.

'Don't take your helmet off,' said Adeola and Akshai together.

'Your other part wants to see you. We, all agree to this. It is efficient.'

'Sarah? Answer me. Don't take your helmet off! We don't know what's in the air. We don't even know if you'll be able to breathe!'

The other voice didn't speak and I knew they were waiting for me.

'Sarah? Sarah? Are you there?'

'I'm here.' I reached around the seal of the helmet, looking for the release mechanism. The clip was a small bump under gloved fingers but it eventually yielded to my clumsy fumblings.

Involuntarily I held my breath as I lifted off the mask even as the comm link buzzed with people asking me to confirm I wasn't taking it off.

The light was more intense without the visor, the emissions bright, sharp enough to make me wince as they left spots on my vision. The air on my skin was thick, as tangible as fog on a cold morning. I didn't immediately die so took a nervous breath, trying to figure out what I'd do if my nostrils started burning or my throat closed up.

It tasted sweet, like lavender and honey, but as it sat in my lungs its edges were burnt plastic and rusting iron.

I held the helmet in my arms, the visor facing outwards so that they could see what I was seeing.

'All, I appreciate your decision,' said a voice that came through the entire Annexe. It had the timbre of a dozen people speaking in harmony, higher and lower pitches timed to give it depth and a richness. It was like talking to an acapella group.

Rhona emerged from the shadows beyond the screen bank. She was wearing the clothes I'd dressed her in except they were riven with thin pulsing threads of lichen. Patches of moss and grass grew at random across them.

'Where do we start?' I asked.

'We, visiting, first, have a protocol that is revealed, followed.'

I smiled. 'So do we.'

A chair grew out of the floor beside Rhona, the sound of it emerging the crack of dead wood in the forest.

'Sit.'

I found another had grown up behind me.

Gingerly lowering myself into the chair I felt it shift underneath me, adjusting to my contours until I realised I'd miss it when I stood again.

'We, all have had time enough to examine your presentation within information space.'

I thought hard about what she said then realised they still lacked the right words to speak simply. 'You mean you've had enough time to understand our biology?'

'That's close to an understanding.'

'And?'

'Your central processing units are very similar to what was expected, experienced before, consistent with theory.'

'You're saying everyone out there has the same type of brain?'

Rhona shook her head. 'No. We expect information to reflect upon itself in certain ways and this is what we find when, in, about you.'

'Are you artificial intelligences?' I stopped. Maybe that wouldn't make enough sense. 'Did someone make you?'

Rhona raised her eyebrows at the question the way she would when showing me a piece and I asked if it was finished. 'No. Intelligence cannot be made except that it resembles you, or us.'

'We're pretty close,' I said. 'We've managed to make AI that taught itself to play our toughest games without any human input. In the reports I've read, the world's best players were quoted as saying it made moves they didn't even understand.'

'Pattern recognition is a slender, if necessary, element of intelligence. Reflective information systems possess convergent forms.'

'You mean they all look the same?' The idea itself was enough for entire research groups to secure funding for the rest of their careers. 'So you dropped by to talk about intelligence? To tell us you have brains as well?'

Rhona shook her head. 'You reached us, our systems, early alerts. So some, I came to observe and meet you. This event will not persist as we, us, all have little intersection with you.'

'You're going to leave?' I said it loudly for the benefit of those listening through my helmet.

'None are here, now, before. Emptiness of us alongside you.'

'What is all this then? Why change everything if you're not really here?' I asked, gesturing at what they'd done to the Annexe, at the grasses that were slowly growing over my feet like cats choosing somewhere inconvenient to sleep.

'These changes accompany our conversation. We cannot control the form information takes for itself. The one hosting we, us remembers beauty this way and it seems effective to show you beauty.'

For sure, Rhona had never seen wild flowers that fluoresced or phosphoresced. It didn't seem true. 'These aren't her memories.'

'Her shape, history, trajectory blurs what is shown, shapes it, but it is always our, my information.' Rhona stood up and, peering down at me, said nothing more.

'Is that it? What did you want to talk to me about?' My fists clenched at the emptiness of it. Everything they'd done seemed meaningless.

'We, us, did not wish to speak with you. We, visiting, first contact, have had the time needed to understand and would depart.'

'Is that it? You won't come back? We don't get to actually meet you? What happens when we rerun our simulations and trigger your systems again?'

'You will not find us, all again until all, we wish to be found. The spaces in which we, you, us met will be cleared for you to follow your path.'

I sank back in the chair, their words gutting me for reasons I couldn't explain. 'And what about me?' I asked, my voice a whisper.

'Sarah,' said Rhona, her voice like it was before she was ill. I lifted my head and saw my love looking back at me. 'I'm why they asked you to come.'

Eleven

There were glints of diamond in her pupils, the promise of glittering stars in the wilderness. She balanced there before me for a moment then her body lost its strength and Rhona sat down heavily, the chair cushioning her fall.

I was out of my seat and by her side before I realised I was moving.

Her name was on my lips, being said again and again. I wanted to hold her close but could see she was in pain, that I had to be gentle.

'It's you. It's really you.' I hid my face in her chest.

Her hands went around me tenderly, touching but oh so fractionally, as if she were afraid of breaking me.

'My love,' she said and stroked my hair. We stayed like that, not for long enough, not by far, but in those moments my heart was fuller than it had been for all the time I could remember.

'We haven't got long,' she said.

'They're going. You'll be back then.'

Rhona shook her head, her chin rubbing against my scalp. 'Sarah, look at me.' I pulled away from her body and forced myself to meet her gaze. 'They told me that I'm dead? That I stopped working before they could do anything about it, that there wasn't anything to be done.'

'They can heal you,' I said with furious hope.

'No. Listen to me. We've got these moments, time until the company comes piling down that corridor to get you. Then. Then you'll go on and find someone else, you'll grow and do even more amazing things.'

'I don't want you to be gone. There has to be something I can do.' I spoke to the room. 'Tell me what I can do. Help me. Help us.'

'Sarah,' said Rhona, tears breaking down her cheeks and sparkling in the light of the room. 'Stop.'

I turned my head, trying to find a focus for what I wanted to say to the visitors. Rhona put her fingertips on my chin, pulling my face back to hers so we could kiss. Our lips together again with her dry, tortured mouth on mine was the sweetest taste in the universe.

We broke away ever so slowly. 'It doesn't matter how we communicate right now, just that we do.' She smiled at me. 'I want you to have no uncertainty about this Sarah Shannon; from me to you with nothing in between – I love you.'

'How can I measure that?' It was the only way I knew how to grasp what she was saying. 'How does what you say reveal that unknown land to me?'

'When did you become so sentimental?' She closed her eyes, a fluttering of her eyelids as she breathed my only clue that her body refused to leave her in peace. The sound of the outer door to the Annexe opening interrupted my thoughts.

'You needed dry land in the storm of my leaving,' she said. 'I get it and I forgive you; you gave me everything I asked for and so much I didn't ask for. I only wish I'd given you my permission to find those things I knew you needed but which I couldn't give you.' She wiped the tears away, a goofy smile holding as she gave all that was left inside. 'I was angry with you for a long time. I thought you would leave me alone just when I needed you the most.'

'I wasn't going anywhere,' I said, the words barely making it onto my tongue.

'I didn't believe it until it was too late. I didn't think I deserved someone so loyal, so amazing.'

'Sarah?' Someone called from across the Annexe.

We both knew they were coming for me. 'They don't understand,' I said, excusing them.

'It's why they won't stay here,' said Rhona.

'Because we're not ready,' I stated and the words felt like they'd wanted to be said for a long time. 'It's such a cliché.'

'I don't think it's that. I remember them in my head, like someone else's memories.' She closed her eyes but in recollection this time. 'Their decisions come from their own mistakes, their own learning. There were so many discussions about us but through all those distinct voices they circled their protocol like a compass seeking true north.'

'Tell me of John Donne,' I said as footfalls approached.

Rhona considered my eyes and began to recite the poem we'd read to one another on our wedding day.

'If they be two, they are two so
As stiffe twin compasses are two,
Thy soule the fixt foot, makes no show
To move, but doth, if the'other doe.'

Other voices called to me but they were nothing compared to her voice. Time slowed as she spoke and the image she conjured of paper into which we were planted, dancing around one another, filled my mind.

'And though it in the center sit,
Yet when the other far doth rome,
It leanes, and hearkens after it,
And growes erect, as it comes home.'

Hands came down on my shoulder, pulling at me as if I were in mortal danger and must be saved at all costs. My body jerked backwards but I kept my head still, refusing to leave until my Rhona was finished. The grass around my feet helped keep me there as her words filled the room. I saw the flowers lighting up at each syllable, the world itself singing to her music.

'Such wilt thou be to mee, who must
Like th'other foor, obliquely runne;
Thy firmnes makes my circle just,
And makes me end, where I begunne.'

Then it gave way and I was pulled into the air, tufts of green coming with me. We had nothing more to say, no opportunity nor meaning we could convey. As the distance between us grew I understood we had spoken everything that could be said, our lives together finished and replete even as time sundered what we had grown.

They lifted me bodily, hands on my arms and legs. I realised I was writhing to be free, to keep looking at my beloved but it was over and such a feat beyond my ability to achieve. Instead I watched the vines along the ceiling give way to the strip lights of the hallway.

A rush of colours, spots of darkness that resolved into eyes and mouths.

'Sarah?'

I couldn't answer them.

'Sarah? Can you hear me?'

I could hear them but what did I have to say. I turned my head away, let it flop to the side, my eyes closing as I remembered that last look, as I attempted to burn it into a memory that would, one day, refuse to recall that moment regardless of any demand I might make of it. I had thought we would reach an agreement, that they would give her back to me.

But they did, I thought, arguing with myself.

All I'd wanted was to find a way to get her home.

'Sarah? Can you hear me? If you can please let us know. Just say "I'm here."'

I opened my eyes to find Adeola's face over mine. 'I'm here.' The words were coffee grounds in my mouth. There were sighs of relief around me. I tried to sit up but hands pushed me back down.

'Let us make sure you're okay.'

But I was okay. 'I'm fine.' I pushed back, determined to sit up. 'Get off me.'

'Sarah, please, let them make sure you're all right.' It was Akshai, pleading with me.

I arced my head to find her and she came into view, I looked like a broken doll in the reflection of her eyes and so for her I stayed still until they were done.

They brought me mint tea, which I loathe. It's hot water that tastes of toothpaste but I was cold and the mug was hot against my fingers as they covered me in silver foil to warm me up.

'You had us worried,' said the Director. She and Akshai were sitting on an operating table across from me. I occupied the other.

'I didn't need rescuing.'

'We found you tangled within a growth of lichen and vines,' said the Director.

'You were staring into space, completely still.' Akshai shivered at the memory of it. 'What happened in there? Why did you take off your helmet?'

'They wanted to talk to me. Surely you saw the footage? I left the helmet where it could see everything I saw.'

Akshai and the Director shared a glance. 'What did you see?'

I frowned at their confusion. 'Rhona. They took Rhona so they could use her to communicate with us. It's why they wanted to speak to me directly I think, because Rhona's emotions, who she was, bled through into their actualisation.'

'It's probably easier to show you,' said the Director.

A woman in military fatigues slid into the room without making a sound and whispered in the Directors ear. When she was done the Director dropped off the operating table, fixed me with a curious expression and said, 'I'd tell you to stay here but you won't listen to me.'

'What's happening?' I was on my feet. Akshai too, looking as worried as I felt, a sense of foreboding playing me like a taut string.

'Our time's up,' she said. I followed her from the tent, Akshai at my back. We crossed the short distance to the main facility and were inside moments later. The daylight made me blink, my eyes sore with the worst hay fever I could imagine.

Where the night before there had been a marketplace of activity, everything was quiet. The computers and equipment were gone while none of the desks, cabinets or other junk they'd pushed to the edges of the atrium had been put back.

We moved through the building to the second floor where a small group of people were protected by two pairs of soldiers carrying rifles that looked frighteningly large.

I saw Adeola directing someone. She stopped, nodded at the Director and focussed on me. 'You're okay.' She sounded genuinely relieved.

Two screens showed the entrance to the lab; people in hazmats were moving large pressurised containers into place.

'Don't attack them' I said.

Adeola looked past me to the Director who shook her head.

'Why? Why attack them? They're leaving.'

'How do you know this?' asked Adeola.

'They told me. They don't want to know us. It was chance we stumbled on them and they came to see what we were. They're done now and are going to clear out so we can't find them again.'

'It doesn't matter, Sarah,' said Akshai at my shoulder. 'You nearly died in there. When we found you, you were in the early stages of hypothermia, covered in grasses that tried to wrap us up as well.' She shook her head as if I were hard of understanding. 'You were dying. Were they helping you then? Were they your friends when you needed them?'

'It's good that they're going,' said the Director.

'We're just going to give them a helping hand,' said Adeola.

'This is a mistake,' I said. 'Just let them go.'

'Okay,' said the Director. 'On one condition; when will they be gone?'

The three women waited for an answer I couldn't give. After a minute the Director spoke again. 'I'm sorry, Sarah. I'm not sure what you experienced in there and I don't know what they said but we won't risk them staying longer than necessary.'

'Don't you get it?' I asked, knowing they didn't. 'Firstly, we can't hurt them. Secondly, they're going anyway and thirdly they're not coming back. They aren't invading, they're not terraforming us. What you saw in there, the wild flowers, the grasses, they were Rhona's memories bleeding through into how they showed themselves.'

'Rhona?' Asked Akshai. 'You saw Rhona?'

The Director stepped between us, her shoulder interrupting our view of one another. 'It doesn't matter. While we're arguing here it's being done.'

The screen showed she was right. Hazmats had cleared the area and at first glance nothing was happening, except as I watched I saw frost crystallising onto the pipes running across the picture and into the Annexe.

'I'm sorry about Rhona,' said the Director.

It was too late for that, she was gone already but none of them had seen her. Why would the visitors hide her from them? It made me look like a woman suffering from a breakdown. It was hard

103

enough to get taken seriously without me recounting conversations with a woman no one else could see.

Adeola hissed a 'yes' as the lichen retreated from the corridor, shrinking back as if burnt. We watched as its thick limbs lifted off the walls and floor, hovered in the air then pulled back out of sight into the Annexe.

'Without energy they're forced to hunker down,' said Adeola.

'It doesn't work like that,' I said, feeling as if all I was doing was repeating the same mantra again and again. 'They don't need energy to be here.'

The screens fuzzed as the signal blinked then went off.

'Shit,' said the Director. She and Adeola hurried from the room. Akshai stood still, her eyes on me.

'I'm going too,' I said to her, challenging her to stop me.

'I know,' she said and in those two words I heard a distance between us as vast as if we stood in different countries. I had no comfort to offer her, no sentiment about how it would be all right, about how we would be okay. Who can see the world for what it is and then make promises like that?

We hurried to keep up with the other two, catching them as they skipped down stairs to get to the corridor into the Annexe. The four of us pulled up as the doors came into view; the air ahead shimmered, thick currents moving like streams of water folding across each other.

Adeola led the way, walking hesitatingly toward the threshold. Each step took us closer to the tropics as the atmosphere grew wetter and warmer until I could have been standing in Singapore in the middle of the afternoon.

The doors to the Annexe were open and from the darkness within we could see flashes of blues and reds, the hurried mess of frantic movement in the shadows. The golden glow that filled the room the last time I'd been here was gone and the loss of such heartening light grieved me. Something rare and wonderful had gone, never to return.

A hot gust blew out of the Annexe, particles and shreds of grass zipping around us like birds lost in a storm. I covered my mouth with the neckline of my sweater. Adeola, at the front of our little group, stood with arm raised before her as if walking into a wall of wind.

'We can't go any further,' said Akshai, falling back.

Adeola took another step, her body lent forwards into the wind.

Without warning it changed direction, pulling back in all the detritus that had been whirling around our heads. Adeola stumbled ahead, one hand going to the floor as she tried to stop from landing flat on her face.

The doors to Annexe slammed shut.

I was sweating from the heat which in those few moments had climbed up into sauna territory. Putting my hand on the wall I snatched it back, shaking my stinging fingers. 'It's hot. The wall's hot.'

The Director wrapped her hand in the end of her jacket and gingerly reached out to the wall. Pulling her hand away she turned back to me. 'We've got to go.' Adeola was on her feet and pushing ahead. 'Adeola. Time to go.'

She stopped but didn't turn around. I understood the urge, knew how badly she wanted to get into the Annexe. The carpet tiles began to curl up at the corners near the doors.

I pushed past the Director and grabbed Adeola by the arm. 'Come on. Trust me, we *have* to go.'

She looked at me then back at the door as if she might still try to get inside. So I tugged at her arm, succeeding only in turning her back half a step. She shook free, her mouth set thin, her fists clenched tight.

She gave the smallest of nods in my direction and we retreated even as paint began to curl and peel from the walls. The lights above us popped but we knew where we were going.

The doors to the Annexe were glowing red by the time we escaped, smoke rising up from the carpet like dirty steam. We didn't look back as we ran from the facility.

Part 5 - Acceptance

Twelve

The fire shouldn't have burnt for long; the facility was mainly concrete and steel with excellent fire suppressant systems. Except the company had brought in not just pressurised tanks of liquid nitrogen but a truck load of other materials, all as part of their plan to contain the Annexe.

The nitrogen tanks exploded as we stood on the road with the rest of the company's team. The corridor to the Annexe blew out, debris scattering across the site with the smallest chunks landing around us as we ducked, too late, behind cars and trucks. It lasted longer than I expected, the sound, the shock of the blast and in the moments after it seemed to me that the whole world stopped to look at what had happened, at what we had done.

I crawled out from my hiding place to find the main facility listing where half the side facing the Annexe had disappeared. In its place were the raw bones of the building; steels and ruptured concrete and the gashes of shattered windows that had only been refit hours before.

Sirens approached from the motorway; the rest of the world would be here soon enough to take over. At that point the company's power would be set aside and the stories would begin as myriad voices tried to understand what had happened.

A trickle of material tumbled down the side of the facility, the sound of concrete crumbling and taking desks, computers and entire floors with it muted, the decay of what we'd built nothing more than the consequences of decisions no one could undo.

The Annexe was still in one piece, its walls had been built to survive exactly this kind of blast; it was in the basic design of a data centre.

'We should move further away,' Adeola said. 'There are some pretty caustic chemicals in the wreckage that you'd be better off not breathing in.'

Fire appliances arrived, officers piling out of them already in full kit with breathing masks hiding their faces. Behind them came police and ambulances, the former to move us back further and the latter to twiddle their thumbs because through luck or extraordinary foresight, no one had been hurt in the explosion.

The Director was swept away to deal with inquisitive arrivals leaving Adeola, Akshai and me to stand around and watch. An hour later she returned. 'We have another office in the town centre. We're going to decamp there while this gets sorted out.' She might as well have been describing a minor fender bender.

'We're just going to let the emergency services into the Annexe?' I asked.

'Of course not. They're going to secure the main offices before they fall down.' She sighed. 'The whole place is going to come down, but that's in the weeks ahead.' The Director took a deep breath, sweeping her hands down from her neck to the base of her stomach. 'Today we make it safe.'

'Was this what you were expecting?' It was a stupid question but I was tired.

The Director scrunched her face up. 'We're alive, so I... Yes. Better than I was expecting.' She laughed, a small chuckle on the edge of hysteria. 'Having a building at the end of it would have been better but we got all the information out, the footage. Proof.'

'Are they gone?' asked Akshai, staring at the Annexe.

'There's only one way to find out,' I said as I started toward the building.

'What are you doing?' shouted the Director. 'Sarah, get back here.'

I didn't look back, instead breaking into a run in case someone decided to intervene.

The doors to the Annexe were shut but hanging on by willpower alone. The brickwork around them was cracked, the mortar broken away leaving behind fracture lines running out on all sides.

I pushed my hand against the surface, the solidity puffing away as dust wherever my fingers touched the door. With a whoof of air the door fell inwards; I jumped back at the same time, suddenly nervous. Inside it was dark, no glowing whispers of life, no warmth to the air.

Behind me Adeola arrived. She didn't say anything, coming to stand next to me so the two of us were both looking into the Annexe.

'They're gone,' I said.

'It worked,' said Adeola. 'We made them leave.'

'They weren't ever here.' I picked my way into the building. The grass mat had died away leaving behind a carpet of blackened fibres woven together like rotting straw.

'You said that before. What did you mean?'

'They could have come here I guess, but they didn't. They said they were like me, like us.'

'Human?'

'No. That they had brains. It was why they could use Rhona as a host.

Moving through the room was no different to traversing an ancient forest. Under our feet were thick roots, dried out leaves and dead flowers. The only difference was that we could once again see the server racks, the metal cages peering through patchy mulch.

'Have you noticed it's wet in here?' I asked Adeola.

'It didn't seem that way on your camera.'

'It wasn't. Humid, alive, but not wet.'

'They weren't here,' said Adeola and I realised she wanted me to continue.

'They changed enough here to talk to us, found a signal booster that could ensure their message reached us in a way we could receive them.' I kicked at a particularly large mound on the floor, it collapsed with a puff of white dust, like a fungi shooting spores when jostled.

'Did you really meet Rhona?'

'None of you saw her, did you?'

'No.'

'I'm hoping her body is still here.' At last we made it around the initial warren of stacks to the centre of the Annexe where the screen bank hung blank from the ceiling. Rhona's chair was empty, the fronds and feelers of lichen stopping short of its legs as if it were poisonous.

The two of us stopped to take it in. 'She's not here,' said Adeola quietly. 'Did they take her with them?'

My heart leapt at the idea but somehow I knew it wasn't true. 'She's all around us, in the lichen, the mess here on the floor. They used her up.'

'But you say you talked to her,' said Adeola, in her voice a sorrow that encompassed my loss and regret for the story I insisted on telling them was true. She was looking at the wreckage and it gave me a moment to stare at her, to take in that she was human too, not just a cypher for the company's goals. At least not any more than I was.

'I talked to something wearing her form. Except at the end. Somehow they gave her back to me at the last. So I could say goodbye. I'm guessing the footage shows me talking to the air.' Adeola's silence was enough to prove my point. 'I won't back down on this.'

Adeola picked up the glass keyboard, turned it over as if looking at a package with something precious inside. 'It won't matter,' she said. 'I'm holding a keyboard turned to moss and glass in a room that spontaneously grew an alien forest. Whether you saw Rhona isn't going to move the dial.'

'How am I going to bury her? How will she even be declared deceased?' The words stung to say but they were no longer forbidden, no longer ideas that could make reality by their utterance. It was too late for that.

'The Director will make things right for you.'

As the voices of firefighters drifted in from outside, it was obvious my future was less than certain. At some point the hospice was going to ring me expecting an answer about Rhona's location and her wellbeing. I had no idea what I was going to say.

With my feet I moved the mush at the base of Rhona's chair to see if anything at all was left, but there wasn't. She'd stopped wearing jewellery months ago and her clothes, along with her body, were gone.

'Sarah, Adeola?' It was the Director.

'We're here,' said Adeola, turning back from the desk, keyboard still in her hands.

The Director appeared from between two racks, a handkerchief held against her mouth and nose. She spoke through the material. 'There are a bunch of people wanting into here. I told them to wait until I gave them the all clear but more senior members of staff than me are coming and it would be better if we were done before they arrived and start to ask awkward questions.'

'More awkward,' I said.

'That too,' she replied.

'I'm almost done.' The second keyboard lay buried under dried lichen which peeled off it in a big platelet. It appeared undamaged, so I pressed one of the keys just in case.

A single screen came on, the image of fundamental equations flashing up and illuminating us with the slenderest light.

'Holy shit, it still works,' said the Director. It was the first time I'd ever heard her curse.

'What is that?' asked Adeola, pointing at a small square image that hadn't been there when we'd first fled the lichen leaving Rhona behind.

It was a rich pink, almost red with thin lines running across it in waves. At first I thought it was fruit, a watermelon maybe. The idea bugged me, twisting in my head as a hook of thought snared my mind but refused to reveal itself.

'What is it? Why would they send us a picture of a watermelon?' Asked Adeola. 'It makes no sense.' Her head was bent over to the side as she tried to see it more clearly.

'It can't be a watermelon,' said the Director. 'It curves the wrong way.' Her index finger traced down the image.

'It's a calf's tongue,' I said, the words coming out on automatic.

'It can't be,' said Adeola. 'It's all wrong.'

The Director continued to examine the image. 'She's right. It is exactly that. Good grief, that's unsettling.'

'How'd you know?' Asked Adeola.

I didn't want to tell them about Rhona's ideas for her last installation; how would it help them understand? 'It's obvious when you spot it. I think the trick is to see through what you want to see for what's really there.'

'You done here?' Asked the Director, suddenly ready to move on now the illusion had been popped.

I wasn't. I could have stayed there forever looking at a calf's tongue. The entropy of my loss had stopped inexorably increasing. Would it ever decrease? I couldn't tell, I suspected not, that to feel less about the absence of Rhona was not a possibility. But somehow I knew it wouldn't keep growing, that I wasn't doomed to a life without warmth.

Walking back into the sunshine, past firefighters discussing how to make the building secure, past police officers holding back a growing crowd of company investigators I wondered what I would do next because suddenly I had nowhere to go after I left the facility, no one to visit and no friends to talk to.

Rhona was gone.

The Director put her hand on my arm and, in a daze, I turned to see what she wanted.

'Sarah,' she said carefully. 'I'm sorry about Rhona.'

'It's okay,' I said, repeating words spoken to a hundred different people on a hundred different occasions and for the first time in three years they weren't entirely untrue.

About the Author

Stewart Hotston lives in Reading, UK. Having completed his PhD in theoretical physics sometime around the dawn of history, Stewart now spends his days working in high finance. He has had numerous short stories published as well as three novels. His latest novel, the political thriller *Tangle's Game*, was published by Rebellion. Stewart also writes reviews for *Sci Fi Bulletin* and more in-depth analysis for *Vector*. When Stewart is not writing or working, he's a senior instructor at The School of the Sword.

NP Novellas

2: Worldshifter – Paul Di Filippo

High-octane SF reminiscent of Jack Vance but wholly Di Filippo in its execution. Klom is forced into a desperate chase across the stars, pursued by the most powerful beings in the galaxy, after he stumbles on a secret in the bowels of an antique ship.

3: May Day – Emma Coleman

Orphaned during wartime at just seventeen, May continues with the silly superstitions her mum taught her. Until the one time she doesn't; at which point something dark and deadly arises, and proceeds to invade her life, determined to claim her as its own...

4: Requiem for an Astronaut – Daniel Bennett

30 years ago, astronaut Joan Kaminsky disappeared while testing an experimental craft powered by alien technology. Now, her glowing figure starts to appear in the sky, becoming a focus for anti-tech cults. One man, who knew Joan, determines to find out why.

5: Rose Knot – Kari Sperring

Kari Sperring, historian and award-winning fantasy author, delivers a gripping tale of love, infidelity, loyalty, misguided intentions and the price of nobility, featuring some lesser known members of Arthur's court: the sons of Lot, the Orkney royal family.

6. On Arcturus VII – Eric Brown

Former pilot and planetary pioneer Jonathan James is lured back to the one place he vowed never to return to: Arcturus Seven. A Closed Planet; a world where every plant and animal is hell-bent on killing you; the place that cost him the life of the woman he loved.

www.newconpress.co.uk

9 781914 953194